RADIGAN AND THE LADY

Radigan looked from Angelina Foley to her three top gunhands, lined up against the bar, waiting to jump him.

"Drinks are on me," Radigan said quietly, and drew his gun. "If you gentlemen aren't drinking by the time I count three, I'll break an arm for each of you."

Angelina was white with anger. "You can't do that!" she said.

"I'd hate to hit a woman," Radigan said.

"You wouldn't dare!"

"If you play games with men," Radigan said, "you'll play by men's rules."

RADIGAN
Louis L'Amour's great story of a man, his land—and a woman.

BENDIGO SHAFTER
BORDEN CHANTRY
BOWDRIE
BRIONNE
THE BROKEN GUN
BUCKSKIN RUN
THE BURNING HILLS
THE CALIFORNIOS
CALLAGHEN
CATLOW
CHANCY
THE CHEROKEE TRAIL
COMSTOCK LODE
CONAGHER
CROSSFIRE TRAIL
DARK CANYON
DOWN THE LONG HILLS
THE EMPTY LAND
FAIR BLOWS THE WIND
FALLON
THE FERGUSON RIFLE
THE FIRST FAST DRAW
FLINT
FRONTIER
GUNS OF THE TIMBERLAND
HANGING WOMAN CREEK
HELLER WITH A GUN
THE HIGH GRADERS
HIGH LONESOME
THE HILLS OF HOMICIDE
HONDO
HOW THE WEST WAS WON
THE IRON MARSHAL
THE KEY-LOCK MAN
KID RODELO
KILKENNY
KILLOE
KILRONE
KIOWA TRAIL
LAW OF THE DESERT BORN
THE LONESOME GODS
THE MAN CALLED NOON
THE MAN FROM SKIBBEREEN
MATAGORDA
MILO TALON
THE MOUNTAIN VALLEY WAR
NORTH TO THE RAILS
OVER ON THE DRY SIDE
THE PROVING TRAIL
THE QUICK AND THE DEAD

RADIGAN
REILLY'S LUCK
THE RIDER OF LOST CREEK
RIVERS WEST
THE SHADOW RIDERS
SHALAKO
SHOWDOWN AT YELLOW
  BUTTE
SILVER CANYON
SITKA
SON OF A WANTED MAN
THE STRONG SHALL LIVE
TAGGART
TO TAME A LAND
TUCKER
UNDER THE SWEET-
  WATER RIM
UTAH BLAINE
THE WALKING DRUM
WAR PARTY
WESTWARD THE TIDE
WHERE THE LONG GRASS
  BLOWS
YONDERING

Sackett Titles by
Louis L'Amour

1. SACKETT'S LAND
2. TO THE FAR BLUE
   MOUNTAINS
3. THE DAYBREAKERS
4. SACKETT
5. LANDO
6. MOJAVE CROSSING
7. THE SACKETT BRAND
8. THE LONELY MEN
9. TREASURE MOUNTAIN
10. MUSTANG MAN
11. GALLOWAY
12. THE SKY-LINERS
13. THE MAN FROM THE
    BROKEN HILLS
14. RIDE THE DARK TRAIL
15. THE WARRIOR'S PATH
16. LONELY ON THE
    MOUNTAIN
17. RIDE THE RIVER

RADIGAN
LOUIS L'AMOUR

BANTAM BOOKS
TORONTO • NEW YORK • LONDON • SYDNEY • AUCKLAND

RADIGAN

A Bantam Book / October 1958

2nd printing . November 1958	6th printing ... February 1969
3rd printing .... March 1961	7th printing ... February 1969
4th printing ... October 1963	8th printing ... October 1969
5th printing ...... June 1967	9th printing .... March 1970

10th printing .... July 1970

New Bantam edition / July 1971

2nd printing ... October 1971	10th printing .. February 1976
3rd printing .. February 1972	11th printing ... January 1977
4th printing ..... June 1972	12th printing .... March 1977
5th printing .. November 1972	13th printing ... August 1977
6th printing .. February 1973	14th printing ..... May 1978
7th printing .. November 1973	15th printing .... March 1979
8th printing ...... July 1974	16th printing . December 1979
9th printing .. September 1975	17th printing ..... May 1980

18th printing ... September 1981

*Photograph of L'Amour by
John Hamilton—Globe Photos, Inc.*

Library of Congress Catalog Card Number: 58-11778

*All rights reserved.
Copyright © 1958 by Bantam Books, Inc.
This book may not be reproduced in whole or in part, by
mimeograph or any other means, without permission.
For information address: Bantam Books, Inc.*

ISBN 0-553-20617-6

Published simultaneously in the United States and Canada

Bantam Books are published by Bantam Books, Inc. Its trademark, consisting of the words "Bantam Books" and the por-
trayal of a rooster, is Registered in U.S. Patent and Trademark
Office and in other countries. Marca Registrada. Bantam
Books, Inc., 666 Fifth Avenue, New York, New York 10103.

PRINTED IN THE UNITED STATES OF AMERICA

27 26 25 24 23 22 21

RADIGAN

one

The driving rain drew a sullen, metallic curtain across the fading afternoon, and beneath his horse's hoofs the earth was soggy with this rain and that of the rains that had gone before. Hunching his big shoulders under the slicker, Tom Radigan was thinking of the warm cabin and the hot coffee that awaited him when he glimpsed the trail across the meadow.

A walking man will kick the grass down in the direction of travel, but a horse with the swinging movements of its hoofs will knock the grass down so it points in the direction from which it has come. What Tom Radigan saw was the trail of a ridden horse that had come down from the lonely hills to the southwest and headed into even lonelier hills beyond his ranch house.

Squinting from under his dripping hat brim in the direction the trail pointed he saw nothing—only a trail that crossed the knee-high grass of the meadow and disappeared into the hills beyond.

"Now what in thunderation," he said aloud, "would anybody want back in there on a day like this?"

Or on any other day, for that matter.

In a world in which most things have a reason, Radigan was disturbed. Northern New Mexico in the 1870s was not a place where men rode for pleasure, and especially not in a driving rain on the heels of several days of driving rain; nor was there anywhere to go in that direction other than the bluff back of the ranch.

Nor was it a riderless horse, for a wandering horse does not move in a straight line nor at the pace this horse had traveled.

Ordinarily, Radigan would not have seen the trail for this was not a route he usually chose, but for the past

months he had been moving stock into a remote area
known locally as the Valle de San Antonio, a well-
watered valley nearly twenty miles from his home
ranch.

Three days ago he had driven a dozen head of cattle
to augment the herd already there, and had remained
long enough to trap and kill two mountain lions who
had begun poaching on his herd—and he had also
killed a cinnamon bear. There were now three hundred
and some head of cattle in the upper valley.

Returning, he found this trail, which could scarcely
be more than an hour old.

Whoever had made the trail had chosen a route that
could not have been accidental; no casual rider would
have come that way, but only someone who did not
wish to be seen. There were easier ways and more direct
routes.

Tom Radigan's R-Bar outfit was remote, hidden
back in the hills far from any accepted route of travel.
He worked his range alone but for one hand, a half-
breed Delaware who had once scouted for the Army
and was known as John Child.

Nothing about that trail or the direction of travel
made sense, and Tom Radigan was a man who was disturbed by the illogical.

Coming out of the draw where the meadow lay he
looked across the fairly wide sweep of Canyon Guadalupe and over the gradually rising bench beyond it toward the ranch. During a momentary lull in the rain
the ranch buildings and the trees around them were
plainly visible, for the ranch was almost three miles
away but a thousand feet higher than his present position.

Uneasily, he studied the ranch, and then bit by bit
he surveyed the intervening country. The route of the
strange rider led across the hills to the north and west,
but mostly to the west.

Nothing in his life gave him reason for a sense of
security, nor had he ever been a reckless man, nor one
given to taking unnecessary chances. He had, even as a

boy, often been accused by the more foolhardy of being afraid to take chances, and the very idea of taking a risk that was not demanded by circumstances was repugnant to him. Yet much of his life had been lived where caution was the price of survival, and being the man he was, he had survived. He did not take chances, but had helped to bury men who did.

So now he took none. He rode slowly, utilizing every bit of terrain that offered cover or concealment, and avoiding his usual route by swinging south of a rocky promontory by a way that ran parallel to the trail.

The problem of the strange rider was disturbing, yet approaching the ranch with care he saw no one. A thin trail of smoke lifted from the chimney, but there was no other movement, and there should have been. Riding in from behind the stables and corrals, Radigan drew up and surveyed the situation with care.

Behind the ranch house which faced him across the clearing, the mesa towered five hundred feet above the low buildings and their surrounding trees. At the base of the mesa Tom Radigan had found that most precious of ranching commodities—water. And he had found plenty of it.

A dozen springs flowed from cracks and caves in the lower wall of the mesa to gather in a pool at its base, and from the pool a small stream trickled off down the mountain to lose itself in Vache Creek some distance from the ranch. Before the water left his own immediate ranch yard Radigan turned it aside to irrigate a small home garden as well as several acres of alfalfa, the first planted anywhere around of which he knew. Leaving the garden and the alfalfa the remaining water trickled into a series of small pools where his stock came to water.

A wanderer and a prowler of the back country, Radigan had come upon an ancient Indian trail that led him to this place. There were no signs of life but wild animals, and a few arrowheads of a kind used by no Indians of the time. There had been no tracks, no evidence of any human visit, so here Tom Radigan built his cabin and corrals. Later, he drove in a small herd of cattle, forty head of cows and two good bulls. He brought with him four mules and three saddle ponies, a small remuda which he augmented by capturing wild horses in the breaks of the mountains to the north where all was utter wilderness for many miles.

It was knowledge of that wilderness which now made him cautious. A man on the dodge running to one of the three or four outlaw settlements reported to exist up there would not have chosen this route, either. Nothing about that rider made any kind of sense—unless he had an enemy of whom he was not aware.

Tom Radigan was a tall, quiet man who rarely smiled except around the eyes, and who talked little but listened well. His was a disconcertingly direct gaze in times of trouble, and men who faced him at such times found that gaze unnerving and upsetting to sudden action. At least such reports had come from three men . . . two others had been in no condition to volunteer any information.

Under the slicker he wore a blue Army shirt faded from many washings and wool pants tucked into Spanish boots. Belted low he wore a Colt six-shooter, and there was enough ammunition in his belt.

Out of Illinois by way of Texas, Tom Radigan was one with those others from Illinois who were to make their mark in the Western country such as Wild Bill Hickok and Long-Hair Jim Courtright. A man with a liking for solitude and a desire to build something stronger than a stack of chips, Radigan had looked for just such a place as he had found here, and he had been careful to choose an area where he was not likely to be disturbed by neighbors.

In the four years at the ranch under the mesa his herds had increased by breeding and purchase. He sold none of his original stock but managed a living and some buying money by trapping and washing gold. The trapping was good in the winters, and the deposits of gold were thin, but the gold was nearly all pure profit for a man with a rifle and a steady hand could live well on the upper range of the Nacimientos and Sangre de Cristo Mountains.

Tom Radigan was a considering man. He took his time to study things out, and he was never one to come to quick decisions or solutions. He took his time now.

Four years of comparative quiet had not lulled his sharpness of sense—his hunting alone would have kept that alive—nor had it made him less wary. There were many reasons why a strange rider might come up the Canyon Guadalupe, but none of which he could think for coming over the rugged mountains to the east of it . . . unless he wanted to approach without being seen. And if he wanted not to be seen he wanted not to be seen by Tom Radigan or his one ranch hand.

A welcoming man, Tom Radigan could think of no reason why anybody should avoid him unless it was an enemy or someone who planned to do him harm.

He sat his saddle for fifteen minutes in partial concealment, his every sense warning him of trouble.

The rain had begun again, but a slower rain now, blotting out the landscape and bringing a chill to the evening. The altitude was 8,700 feet and winter was closing in.

The rain could turn to snow at any time, and the forest to the north would be closed to any traveler. His route to the settlements below was only occasionally closed, and it was downhill all the way, yet most travel would be ended with the first good fall of snow.

He scowled, watching the house, the hills, the forest and the mesa rim.

If an enemy or some chance thief who needed supplies and a fresh horse wanted to kill him that thief would be watching the trail up which he had not come. The yard before the barn was visible only from the rim of the mesa and the talus slope behind the house. But his approach was safe until within a step or two of the barn door, and if he moved with care . . .

The gelding stamped impatiently and Tom Radigan swung down and opened his slicker, moving his Colt into an easier position. Then, remaining on the side of the gelding that kept the horse between himself and any marksman on the talus slope, he went around and into the stable.

His first thought was for the horse. Stripping off the saddle and bridle, he rubbed the animal down with a piece of sacking, his mind turning over all the possible facets of the situation. He was probably being a fool; the rider might have been someone lost and searching for shelter.

Yet there was no sound from the house, and John Child did not appear, as he usually did. It was the half-breed's custom to stroll out from the house, help him with the horse and exchange gossip about the activities of the day.

Through the partly opened door he studied the house. By this time it would be dark inside and John would have lighted a lamp . . . you'd never catch John Child moving around in a dark house of his own free will.

Yet John's horse was in his stall, and his saddle in its proper place. So why had not John come to greet him, and why wasn't the light lit?

He might have walked away afoot, but that was unlike John who never walked farther than from the house to the corral or stable. He might be inside the house and sick or injured . . . the only alternative was that John was trying to warn him of something.

A warning of what?

The situation at the ranch now seemed part of the sequence of affairs begun with the strange trail across the meadow. Never a trusting man, Tom Radigan had lived by taking care, and if someone were in the house waiting for him they would be apt to have the light going to make the situation as normal as possible. And the mud around the door had few tracks . . . he studied those tracks again.

Somebody had come out and gone back. The steps from the house were even and regular until the fourth step which was skidded sharply in the slippery mud, and the returning steps were longer. Whoever had come out of the door had started toward the barn, had wheeled and sprang back for the house.

It was very quiet. There was no sound but the falling rain.

Nothing in the house could have made John Child turn and rush back so suddenly so it had to be something outside.

So then: there was nothing in the barn to frighten John, nor was there cover for an enemy to the east and northeast. There was cover from the southwest, the way Radigan had come, but Radigan had seen no tracks there.

That left two possible places and one so remote as to be out of the question, but the second place tied in with that unknown rider.

Nobody could have shot at John from the rim of the mesa because nobody knew the way up there but John and himself, but a shot fired from the talus slope back of the house would have found a target at just about the point where John had wheeled and dashed back into the house.

All right, that was it, then. Somebody was or had been on that talus slope behind the house, and that somebody might still be there waiting for a shot at John or himself the instant one of them appeared in the open yard. Approaching from the southwest as he had, Radigan would not have been visible from the slope, not until he had been right by the barn door. Nor would he be visible again until his second or third step out of the barn.

Radigan could wait where he was until it was full dark, which might be no more than a half hour, or he could go now and risk a shot.

Whoever had fired that shot—if there had been a shot—undoubtedly wanted to kill him and not John Child, or he wanted both of them.

Yet this was purely supposition. Nothing at all might be wrong.

Nothing in his life had given him reason to take chances. From Illinois he had gone to Kansas where he served his apprenticeship as a military man with General Lane during the bloody fighting in that border state, and from there he had gone to Sante Fe as a freighter, surviving two savage Indian attacks. For two bloody years he had fought Comanches in Texas. It was the sort of conditioning to make a man careful.

He was reasonably sure there had been trouble, and even at this moment John might be lying inside the house badly hurt. It would do John no good to get himself killed trying to help him, and the surest way to help John was to eliminate the danger.

Drawing back inside the barn he squatted on his heels and lighted a cigarette. If a man were to hide on that slope there were a dozen possible places, but none of them would conceal a horse.

So the sniper's horse would be hidden down in the trees on the lower hill, and somewhere east of the ranch. There was no cover directly east of the ranch yard, but around the corner of the hill there were scattered clumps of trees and brush, and then lower down, thick forest. The rifleman had hidden his horse somewhere down the slope and then had crawled up in the talus where he could cover the ranch yard.

Within the hour it would be completely dark.

After dark there would be no reason for anyone to wait up on that slope for there would be nothing to see. Therefore the hidden man would return to his horse and ride off somewhere to give up or await a better chance the following day.

Not even a mouse trusts himself to one hole only, and Radigan was no mouse. In the side of the barn that formed one wall of the corral there was another door made of sawed logs that was perfectly fitted and left for emergencies. He had never used that door since it had been built, but now he did.

Easing himself out that door, which was invisible from any place the watcher could be, he went down the slope behind the barn and into the trees. On a run, he began to circle the ranch area to get where a horse might be concealed. Pausing for breath in a clump of trees he told himself he was a fool—the half-breed had probably gone off somewhere.

But where? His horse was in the barn, it was raining, there was no reason of which he could think for Child to leave the house . . . and where had that strange rider disappeared to?

A watcher on that slope, if he wished to kill from ambush, must have his horse close in case something went wrong, which left four possible places of concealment. One was a wash where the runoff from the slope had cut a deep gash in the earth, another was a nest of boulders, the third a patch of brush, and the fourth a notch in the rocky face a hundred feet down from the bench on which the ranch stood. That notch could give easy access to the talus slope, and a horse waiting below it would provide a fast escape.

Rain fell steadily, and slight wind stirred the leaves, whipping cold rain down his neck. He held his rifle muzzle down beneath his slicker, from which he had slipped an arm to hold the Winchester, as he worked his way to a new vantage point.

It was almost dark and at any moment the man might be returning to his horse. Every stop Radigan took was now a danger, and he made no move without checking the terrain before it.

Far up the slope, a stone rattled.

Darting across a small open space he reached the nest of boulders, but there was no horse, no tracks. There was little time, and as the crack in the rock seemed the most likely place, he tried it next.

Rain whispered on the leaves, the world was gray and black now, shaded by rain and the coming of night.

He paused in the shadow of a boulder, his feet on the sand of a gradual slope. He worked his way through the trees, and the ground was soggy beneath his boots. Raindrops felt his cheeks with blind, questing fingers . . . the black trunks of the trees were like iron bars against the gray of gathering pools.

Alert, nostrils distended, every sense reaching into the night, testing the air for what it held, he waited, and there was no sound. Walking on, he rounded the corner of a rocky promontory and saw the horse.

Standing head down, partly sheltered by the overhang, it waited.

He had been right, then.

He stood close beside a sentinel pine, holding his body to merge with the blackness of the trunk. It was dark now.

Rain talked to the leaves. No bird moved—birds and rabbits were wise enough to take shelter when it rained. The horse stood disconsolate in the rain, and the rocks were black and wet.

It was cold . . . he relaxed his grip on the gun action and shifted his hold. The crack in the rock merged its blackness with the surrounding dark so he could scarcely distinguish the opening, but the horse shifted its feet and the saddle glistened wetly.

A boot scraped on stone, a pebble cascaded among the rocks.

Delicately, Radigan tilted the Winchester barrel up to meet his left hand. He held the gun at hip level, ready to lift it for a quick shot.

There was a moment of silence, then a boot crunched on sand. A dark figure moved the shadows in the mouth of rock, and in the moment before the man reached the horse, Radigan said, "You looking for somebody?"

The man twisted and the flat stab of fire thrust toward him from the darkness and the rain, crossing the heavier sound of his Winchester, firing almost of its own volition, an instant late. He felt the shock of the bullet as it hit the tree beside him and spattered his face with tiny fragments of bark.

He fired a second time, realizing as he did so that the other man was fast, and a dead shot. Without warning more than his words the man had wheeled and fired . . . he saw the man's body crumpling to the sand and the horse shy back, snorting. Tom Radigan moved a bit more behind the tree and waited.

He was not about to run up to a man shot down, or seemingly shot down. He waited without movement, listening to the slow whisper of falling rain: there was no other sound.

The horse blew through his nostrils, not liking the smell of gunsmoke. A wind stirred the corner of Radigan's slicker.

The shot was a dart of red flame and a smashing concussion. A finger tugged at the slicker and Radigan fired, levered the Winchester and fired again into the dark bulk of the body.

Silence again, and rain. It was dark, but his eyes were accustomed and he could make out the body against the gray sand.

He waited, feeling sure the man was dead . . . this time he was dead.

Who had he killed? What was the man doing here, far from any other ranch or town? How had he even known about this place? In the four years since Radigan came to the bench above the Vache there had been no more than a half-dozen visitors.

The man had come to kill, or else he would not have fired so suddenly at a strange voice speaking from the darkness. And he had been a man skilled in the use of arms, arriving by a route he must have known or to which he must have been well guided.

The minutes dragged, and Radigan waited. Many times the first man to move was the first to die, and he had learned patience. After awhile there was a short, convulsive sigh and a boot toe scraping in the sand. The man was dead.

Radigan moved to another tree, his rifle held ready for another shot.

Near the white palm of an outflung hand Radigan saw the wet shine of a pistol barrel. He came from behind the tree and walked toward the body. The tied horse, not liking the mingled smell of powder smoke and blood, backed off, snorting softly.

"Easy, boy. Easy now."

The horse quieted, reassured by the calm voice. Radigan had a way with animals—they trusted him.

Even the bad ones seemed to buck under him merely to uphold their reputations, but with no heart in it.

Radigan prodded the body with his toe, rifle held for a shot, and when there was no move he turned the body so the face lay white under the dripping sky.

Squatting near the body, Radigan felt for a pulse and found none. Spreading his slicker, he struck a match under its shelter, and looked at the dead face, mouth slightly open, eyes wide to the rain.

Young—not more than twenty-one or -two. A narrow face with a hard mouth and thin lips, a forehead too high. The holster was slung low and tied fast.

Lifting the body, Radigan draped him over his saddle, then retrieved the rifle and pistol and leading the horse he walked back to the barn.

As he entered the yard the door opened and John Child stepped out with a lantern.

Child took the dead man's head in his grip and turned the face to the light. "Know him?"

"No . . . do you?"

"No, I don't. Something familiar there, though."

Radigan noticed a small patch of bandage on Child's skull and indicated it with his eyes. "He hit you?"

"Burned me. I had your coat on." He looked at Radigan across the darkness. "What's the matter, Tom? What's wrong?"

"Damned if I know." He explained about the tracks that came over the hills far from any trail, indicating the man had come with purpose in mind, using a way that would avoid the chance of being seen. "Somebody hunting me, John. Or you."

Child considered that. "You," he said finally. "My enemies are dead." He looked at the body. "Bury him in the morning?"

"No. I'm a curious man, John. A wanting-to-know sort of man. I'm going to leave him tied across that saddle and turn the horse loose."

There was a moment of silence while the rain fell, and then Child muttered, "Damn!" There was wonder and satisfaction in his tone. "I'd not have thought of that."

"Maybe, just maybe it'll work. The horse might be borrowed or rented, but it might be his own. In any case, that horse is likely to go home. Or maybe to where it was fed and stabled last."

"You'll do," Child said. "You'd have made a fine Indian, Tom."

He studied the body, noting the three bullet holes. "He was a tough man."

"And fast," Radigan said. "He was fast and he was good. He was awful good. Two shots in the dark, one hit the tree I stood against, the other nicked my raincoat. This was a man knew his business, John. He was a man hired for the job. I'm guessing."

"Who?"

That was the question, of course. From time to time a wandering man made enemies, but none that mattered and none who would come this far off their trail to hunt him down. It made no kind of sense, just none at all.

He swore suddenly. "John, we're a couple of children. Give me that lantern."

He held the light up to the brand. It was a Half-Circle T—no brand he had ever head of. Then he pulled the dead man's coat loose and searched the pockets, but there was only a little money, no wallet, no letters. Yet the man had come from somewhere and behind his coming there was a reason.

"Tom." Child waited a moment while the time ran and the rain fell. His voice was very serious. "Tom, you be careful. Whoever wants you took no chances on leaving evidence. He's clean. No identification. They took no chances of him being caught or killed."

"They didn't think about the horse."

"No, but the horse is strange around here. That's no brand we know."

"No, but this horse was fed somewhere, watered somewhere. This here is a grain-kept horse, and I'm gambling this man has been around a day or two, studying the lay of the land, and his horse might go back to where he was fed."

"In the morning?"

"Now. We'll let him start now, and in the morning I'll trail him down." Radigan indicated the sky. "Look —the rain is breaking. The tracks will still be there."

Leading the horse to the trail south he slapped him hard across the rump, and stood while the horse jumped away and then trotted off down the trail, the dark bulk of the dead man in the saddle. They watched him and listened until they could no longer hear the slowing *clop-clop* of the horse's hoofs. Without words they turned and went into the house and Tom Radigan suddenly realized he was tired, dead tired.

"Coffee's on. It'll be stronger than hell."

"What else?"

"Beans, beef . . . what d'you expect?"

Child put down the lantern and lighted a coal-oil lamp. Radigan hung his hat and slicker on wooden pegs driven into the wall and glanced toward the fire. He had been thinking about that fire for a long time.

The room was long with a huge fireplace on one side, and a beamed, low ceiling that cleared Tom Radigan's head by no more than a few inches. It was a frontier room, but somehow more pleasant.

There had been a lot of years when he had thought of a place like this. It lacked a woman's touch, but it was strongly built and comfortable, built to last as Radigan had planned it during the long nights on night herd. It had a view down the valley, and was built for strength and a good defense, for there was always a chance of needing that in a strong new country where men did not readily settle into the ways of law. But there were windows with wide, deep sills, windows that would someday carry plants . . . geraniums, maybe. And there was an inside pump, good for defense, of course, but good also for a woman. It would save her steps and time. It was a rare thing in this country to have an inside pump.

"Got myself a couple of cats," Radigan commented.

"Lose any stock?"

"Over a time, maybe four or five head. These lions were latecomers, I figure. But no lion ever had any sense. Got them both in the same trap, just reset it. Caught them in the same place on successive nights. Never do that to a wolf."

John Child was a square-shouldered man, dark and strong-boned, a man who looked as if he were hewn from oak. The Indian in him was strong, but the white man in him had made him painstaking in his work. He dished up the food, steaming from the fire, and then poured coffee. "You set up to the table, Tom. You're about done in."

Radigan rolled up his sleeves revealing the white skin of powerful forearms, the brown of his hands resembling gloves by comparison. He bathed carefully, working up a good lather with the homemade soap. He washed his face, digging his soapy finger into his ears, then dampened a towel and went behind his ears and finally combed out his stiff brown-red hair. And all the while he was thinking, backtracking himself across the days to find some clue to the unknown dead man and the why of his coming to the ranch on the Vache.

He dropped into a chair almost too tired to eat. In the past few days he had ridden more than a hundred miles, rounding up cattle, moving them to new range, cleaning water holes, branding a few late calves, then trapping lions and killing a cinnamon bear.

"Forgot," he said, "there's bear meat on the saddle."

"It'll keep in this weather."

"Ever eat lion?"

"Sure, many a time. Best meat there is. First time I heard that from a white man was from Kit Carson, down to Lucien Maxwell's place, but the mountain men favored it above anything else."

Child filled his own cup and sat down. "Don't you gorge yourself. There's more."

"You make a pie?"

"No."

Radigan lifted his head and scented the air. "Bear sign?"

"Figured you'd smell 'em first off. When you didn't I knew you were tired. Ma used to make doughnuts when I was a youngster and when I'd come from school I'd catch that smell, even if it had been hours old."

"You get me some, John. You ain't much for work, but I'd keep you on just for making bear sign. I never saw your beat."

"Time was I've been kept making bear sign for three days without letup, make 'em by the dishpan full, and none left at the end. Men ride miles to get a handful of bear sign."

They were silent, busy with their food and thoughts. Only Radigan was eating, however. After a few minutes he asked, "You eat?"

"Sure. I'd started out to feed the stock when that feller nicked me. First off I was of a mind to go scalp huntin', but he had me nailed down so I ate . . . first thing I was taught was to sleep whenever there was time and to eat when there was food."

John Child went to the deep cupboard and brought back a plate of doughnuts. "Dig in boy. There's a plenty."

"John . . . who d'you reckon he was?"

"Gunman, that's for sure. Trigger tied back on his gun. And a mighty fine rifle. He's got to be a hired killer."

Tom Radigan took down his rifle and went to work cleaning it. As he worked he occasionally ate bear sign and drank coffee.

It had been too good to last. He owned seven hundred head of cattle, and a nice bunch of mustangs. He had spread his cattle around through the mountain meadows where there was good water and good grass, and from time to time he shifted his small herds to new areas where the grass was still long. The winters were vicious, and the snow drifted deep in most of the canyons. It was a brutal struggle to keep the herds alive but there were areas where the wind swept the grass free of snow, and there were protected valleys where little snow gathered. There had been natural increase, and several times he bought cattle from movers. As there were no other ranches close by and the remote valleys restricted the wandering, the task of handling the cattle was a small one.

Radigan's progress had been steady, and in another year he would make his first drive to market. His income from trapping was sufficient to pay Child his wages and to put by a little, and from the first he had taken time out occasionally to wash out a little gold from the streams. None of them carried much, but to a man whose wants were simple it was enough.

The ranch on the Vache had been no sudden thing. From the first he had made up his mind to look for just the place he wanted, and when he found it his plans were well made and he was ready for the hard work they demanded. Every step he must take had been carefully planned, and he believed he had covered all the possible risks and chances to be expected. From the beginning he had been aware that the days of free range could not last, and he had never planned on the vast operations of the bigger ranchers. He was content with a small outfit but one that paid well, and he had solved the problem of making it pay.

At daybreak he was out of bed and into his socks and shirt. Then he stirred the coals and laid on a few chunks of pitch pine to get a hot fire going, then he put on the water for coffee.

When he had bathed and dressed he took time out to shave, the wiry stubble on his jaws yielding reluctantly to the razor. He was usually clean-shaven except for his mustache—his one vanity.

John Child came in. "Saddled that blaze-face sorrel for you. It's clearing up nicely."

"Thanks."

"Want I should ride along?"

"Stick around. There's enough to do and I don't

want the place left alone now. You keep your guns close and don't get far from the place."

Child grinned at him. "I'm a Delaware . . . you forgettin' that?"

"It's the English in you worries me. The Delaware can take care of itself."

"I've put up a lunch . . . and some of them bear sign."

Radigan shouldered into a buckskin coat and went down to the corral. The sorrel was a good trail horse, half-Morgan and half-mustang, with lots of bottom and enough speed.

He stepped into the leather and Child put a hand on the saddle. "You watch yourself. That dead man's face is something I remember and I remember it with trouble."

No need to worry, Child told himself. Radigan was a good man in woods or mountains, and like an Apache on a trail. He had been a Texas Ranger for two years and built a solid reputation, but he was not a man to shoot unless pushed into it.

The trail was plain enough, for there had been a hard rain that wiped out tracks before the shooting and wind enough to dry the mud and set the tracks since the rain stopped. The horse had galloped a short distance, settled to a canter and then to a walk. Several times it had hesitated as if uncertain, then had set out down the trail. The trail led right to the bottom of Guadalupe Canyon and after that there was small chance to wander.

San Ysidro was nothing much as a town. Three stores, two saloons and a third saloon that was called a hotel because they occasionally rented rooms, and a scattering of houses, most of them adobe. It was just short of noon when Tom Radigan rode into town.

There were four horses at the hitching rack and a buckboard, but nobody on the street.

Three of the horses were branded with a Running M-on-a-Rail, a brand strange to him. He tied his horse at the hitching rack and went into the saloon. Two of the men at the bar were strangers, the third was Deputy Sheriff Jim Flynn and the fourth a man in buckskins who trapped over in the Nacimientos. His name was Hickman.

They nodded to each other and Flynn asked, "Travelin', Tom? Didn't figure to see you around here this late in the year."

"Man has to get out, time to time." He glanced briefly at the two strange riders. They looked to be tough, competent men. But why here? There was no Running M-on-a-Rail in this part of the country and no open range. There should be a third rider . . . where?

Deputy Sheriff Flynn was doing some thinking of his own. He had been marshal of two cowtowns, sheriff and deputy sheriff elsewhere, and as far as he was concerned San Ysidro was the end of the line. He was married now and the father of two children, and he wanted no trouble here.

A handy man with a gun who knew his job thoroughly, he had always been worried by Tom Radigan.

He had known such men before. Hickok and Courtright, of course, but Radigan was more like Tilghman, Gillette or John Hughes. He was a dangerous man, but a man with quality, tempered in harsher fires than San Ysidro could offer.

A quiet man, Radigan minded his own business and rarely drank, but Flynn understood the potential. Knowing his business as he did he also knew there was no logical reason for Radigan's presence in town today. Radigan had bought supplies only two weeks ago and they usually lasted him all of two months, but this had been an order for the winter and unusually heavy. Nor did Radigan come to town for company or to get drunk. The deputy sheriff took another look at Radigan's face and decided this was a war party.

Toying with his glass, he estimated the situation. What had happened that was different than usual? What could have happened to bring Tom Radigan into town right now?

The answer was obvious. The three strange cowhands

and the stranger with the buckboard. All were armed, all looked to be tough, capable men; and more than that, they were better dressed, hence better paid. These were not simply cowpunchers but fighting punchers. And fighting men are not hired unless to fight.

"Stage is about due," Flynn commented.

"No rush this time of year," Downey the barman said as he leaned his thick elbows on the mahogany. "Folks just naturally start avoiding this country just shy of first snowfall, and they're smart."

One of the strange riders looked around. "Does it get cold here?"

Flynn nodded, looking into his glass. "You're up high, man. You're right near a mile above sea level here, and any place out of town it's higher." He indicated Radigan with a jerk of his head. "Up at Tom's place it's a half-mile higher. And *cold?* Seen it forty below up there, many a time."

The door opened then and a big man came in. As tall as Radigan's six feet and two inches, he was thirty pounds heavier than Radigan's one hundred and eighty-five. His square, powerful head sat on a wide thick neck and powerful shoulders, yet for all his beef he moved easily, and he glanced sharply at Radigan, then again.

"I know you from somewhere," he said.

"Maybe."

"You live around here?"

The cowhands had straightened up at the bar and so had Flynn. "Could be."

The newcomer hesitated as if to say something further but a shrill yell from down the street and the rattle of hoofs and harness brought the stage up to the door.

Flynn, Radigan thought, was relieved, but he made no move toward the door until the three cowhands had gone out. The big man stood in frowning concentration, then called after the last man through the door. "Coker," he said, "shake the snow off those robes in the buckboard."

Radigan glanced out the window. It was snowing, not very seriously, but snowing nonetheless. He felt relieved. A good snow now might close the country for all winter. His first glance registered the snow, but the second caught the horse tied behind the stage.

Hickman stepped in the door. "Sheriff," he said, "we've a dead man out here."

Downey came from behind the bar. All of them went out but Tom Radigan. He refilled his glass.

Hickman glanced at him curiously. "Ain't you curious?"

"Me?" Radigan glanced at him. "I've seen a dead man."

He tossed off his drink and stared at his glass, wondering why he ever touched the stuff. He didn't really like it and he had discovered long ago that it took a lot to have any effect on him and when he got the effect he didn't like it.

The door pushed open and men came in carrying a body which they stretched on the pool table. The big man followed them in, his features a study in puzzled anger. A man obviously the stage driver entered with Downey and Flynn.

"About ten mile out," the driver was saying, "we come around a bend and there was this horse, walkin' toward us. We figured it was somethin' for you."

The deputy sheriff stared sourly at the dead man. Why didn't they let the horse keep going? Clean out of the county? "Anybody know him?" he asked.

Nobody spoke up. In the silence Hickman glanced quizzically at Radigan. Flynn noted the glance.

"He's some shot up," Downey commented, "and I'd say early last night." At Flynn's questioning glance Downey flushed. "Worked with doctors durin' the war," he said. "I know something about wounds."

"He could have come quite a ways," Flynn commented, "since early last night."

Tom Radigan was sure he knew what Flynn was thinking, that the unknown dead man could have come from the ranch under the mesa. There were not too many places he could have come from except maybe Jemez or Jemez Springs. Deputy Sheriff Flynn, Radigan decided, was no fool.

"All the wounds are in front," Radigan commented.

"That's where you'd expect 'em to be," Hickman said. "That's Vin Cable."

Flynn turned sharply around. "Damn it, Hickman!" he demanded irritably. "What would Vin Cable be doing up here? He's a warrior, a dollar-on-the-barrelhead fighting man."

Hickman shrugged. "How should I know what he was doin' here? Maybe somebody is startin' a war?"

"Cable must've killed five or six men," Downey said.

"That folks can testify to," Hickman added. "No tellin' how many he dry gulched."

The big man turned sharply on Hickman. "You talk a lot," he said.

"You don't like it?" Hickman's voice was mild. He was idly whittling with a bowie knife.

"Stop it," Flynn said, glaring at him. The deputy looked as sore as a hound dog with a bad tooth. He smelled trouble, Radigan surmised and, good officer that he was, wanted to avoid it.

Coker came to the door and called to the big man, "Ross, Miss Foley is ready to go."

Radigan followed them to the street, and Flynn trailed after.

A tall young man was helping a girl in a gray traveling dress from the stage. She had dark-brown hair and, as Radigan saw when she glanced up at him, green eyes. He escorted the girl to the buckboard and paused there as Ross joined them. Whatever he said caused the young man to turn on him, startled and angry. The girl waited, listening.

Flynn seemed to make up his mind. "You folks planning to settle around here?"

Ross turned squarely around to face him. "We do. We've rented the Hansen place until our cattle come in, and then we're moving up on Vache Creek."

Flynn started to speak but Radigan interrupted. "I wouldn't count on it," he said.

All eyes were on Radigan.

"And why not?" Ross demanded.

"Because he missed," Radigan said quietly.

two

The wind skittered a dry leaf along the boardwalk and one of the stage mules, shifting his weight, jangled the harness. Radigan's three words hung in the still, cold air, a challenge issued and a line drawn.

The man who was helping the girl into the buckboard turned his face toward them. "What's that mean?" he demanded.

His was a lean, handsome face with a hint of repressed savagery behind it that Tom Radigan had seen in faces before. There was impatience in such men, impatience that could lead to trouble, impatience that might get them killed or lead to the killing of others.

"My name is Radigan. The R-Bar is my outfit and the R-Bar is Vache Creek."

"I'm afraid you don't understand." It was the girl speaking, and her cool, cultured voice seemed to be merely tolerating stupidity in one who knew no better. "We own twenty-two sections along Vache Creek."

"Along Vache Creek," there was no yielding in his tone, "there is but one ranch and room for but one. I own it."

She arranged her skirt with one casual hand, and the smile went no farther than her lips, lips that were a shade too thin, eyes that were too cool and measuring. "You are mistaken, sir. I am sorry for you, of course, but men who squat on land that does not belong to them must expect to be moved off. That land has been in my family since 1844."

"And you were so sure of your title that you sent your insurance on ahead?"

Ross Wall took a quick, belligerent step forward. "What's that mean?"

"Read it any way you like." Ross was the dangerous one at the moment and Radigan's eyes held on him. The foreman was a fighting man, and he looked a hardheaded man who would take some convincing. "An outfit that sends a gunman ahead of them can't have too much confidence in their title."

"You accusing us?"

"Vin Cable didn't come here for fun. He didn't take a shot at my *segundo* for fun and, from all I hear, he was a man who commanded a high price. I think he was paid insurance that there'd be no argument about titles."

Flynn interposed. "Tom, we'd better look into this. After all, if they have a title—"

"Any title they have isn't worth the paper it's written on." Radigan was brusque. "Moreover, there isn't range enough in Guadalupe Canyon to winter a jack rabbit, and the only range on Vache Creek is my range. There will be no cattle along that creek whose brand does not read R-Bar."

Hickman stood with one foot against the wall, a lean man in soiled buckskins who listened with cynical amusement.

The girl spoke again. "I am Angelina Foley. The land along Vache Creek is part of my father's estate, and the terms of Governor Armijo's grant are clear. No doubt you have made improvements on the land." She opened her purse. "I am prepared to pay for those improvements, and to buy what stock you have."

"That's fair," Flynn said quickly. "How about that, Tom?"

"The land is mine. It will remain mine. If you had taken the trouble to inquire in Santa Fe you would know the status of any grants by Armijo."

For the first time Ross Wall looked uncertain. He glanced at Angelina Foley, awaiting her lead, for obviously this was something for which he had no reply.

"Would you fight a woman, Mr. Radigan? I thought Western men more gallant."

There was no yielding in Radigan. "When you

opened the ball," he replied, "you called the tune.
Anybody, man or woman, who comes hunting a bullet
title to my land is going to have to prove title with
more than conversation. And a woman who takes cards
in a man's game holds the status of a man and is
entitled to no more respect."

"Now, see here!" Flynn said angrily. "You've no
proof of connection between Vin Cable and this lady!
None at all! You just back up on that! Back up, d' you
hear?"

Abruptly, Radigan turned and walked back into the
saloon. The body of Cable had been removed from the
billiard table to a back room where it was partly visible
lying on another table.

Jim Flynn followed Radigan into the saloon and
leaned on the bar beside him. "Have a drink, Tom?"
Flynn tried to speak casually.

"I have one. Thanks."

"Too bad . . . tough time to lose a place, winter
coming like this."

Radigan shot Flynn a hard glance, but made no reply.

"If I were you I'd talk to these people, and try to
work out a deal. Their herd is already on its way here."

"What's got into you, Jim? Are you deputy sheriff of
the county or their lawyer? That land is mine. I've lived
on it and worked it and have an air-tight title. You
don't suppose I'm going to be pushed off my land with
a bluff like that, do you? You'd better decide where
you stand, Jim."

Flynn's face flushed with dark blood. "I stand for
the law, and I'll enforce the law! You put that in your
pipe and smoke it!"

"Seems to me," Hickman commented mildly, "that
Radigan's case is the best one, Jim. He's been in possession four years we know of. He says he's got an
air-tight title. Was I you, Jim, I'd give that some
thought."

Hickman's interference angered him, yet there was
sense in what he said. Still, Flynn told himself, it was

unreasonable that such people could be bluffing, or
that such a girl could be dishonest. These were quality
. . . he had seen it at first glance, and he was a man
who had been taught respect for decent women. The
idea that an educated, intelligent lady would have a
hand in anything shady was beyond consideration. Nor
would an outfit of this size have come here without
having a clear title. Like many another man he had
respect for money and power, and these newcomers
showed every indication of both.

"A girl like that wouldn't lie," Flynn said.

Radigan had no humor in his smile. "If you can say
that, Jim, you've been lucky in the women you've
known."

The door opened and Angelina Foley came in with
Ross and the younger man.

"I am asking you again, Mr. Radigan, to vacate the
premises on Vache Creek."

He turned to face her. "Somebody's misled you, ma'-
am. Have you ever seen this land you claim? Have you
any idea what you're getting into? Guadalupe Canyon
runs north of here, and rim to rim it'll vary from maybe
a half-mile to a mile. In the bottom it isn't anywhere
more than a few hundred yards wide, and nowhere
along that canyon is there graze for a herd.

"North of there it narrows down and sometimes in
the winter we're snowed in for a month at a time, one
time it was three months. In the summer that country
will carry quite a few cows in the high meadows, but to
winter cattle up there calls for a special brand of know-
how that no Plains country puncher will learn in a
season. Most places folks will tell you a man who
tries to winter cattle a mile and half above sea level is
crazy.

"I'd say, ma'am, that you've been poorly advised to
bring a herd up here at this season. My advice would
be to head out of here for the nearest fort or reservation
where they're buying cattle for the Indians and sell out.
After you've spent a winter here, if you still want a

piece of this country, you can find a piece that's not already taken."

"My land is on Vache Creek, Mr. Radigan," she replied coolly. "I am asking you to vacate in the presence of witnesses. If you do not, well, I'm afraid my men won't take kindly to your being in the way of ranch operations."

"Seems odd," Radigan said quietly, "that you'd come into a cold country in the late fall knowing you'd built no buildings on the land. Looks like you knew about mine and figured to have me out of them. Seems you should know you have to feed stock part of the winter, and yet you bring a herd up here. Figuring to use my feed, too? Was that why Vin Cable came first?"

Jim Flynn's brow puckered and he glanced at Angelina Foley, his eyes registering doubt for the first time. It was a telling point, and any man who had grown up around cattle would recognize the logic of it.

She turned toward the door, then glanced back. "You have heard what I said. You have been notified to vacate. When my herd arrives, we will move onto the land."

The batwings swung to behind them, and there was silence in the saloon and stage station.

"There's six men here," Hickman advised, "and there must be a dozen or more with the herd. I'd say you'd chosen yourself a fight."

"I've one man worth a dozen of these, plenty of grub and more than a thousand rounds of ammunition. If it's war they want they've come to the right place."

He downed his drink and turned to the door. It was time he started back. The few flakes of falling snow had disappeared, but the suggestion remained in the air, and the sky above was flat and cold.

At the door Hickman's voice stopped him. "Jim," the trapper suggested mildly, "there's a thought behind this. Now these folks have a right smart outfit. Good horses, good clothes, good rigs. Wonder why they left wherever they were? Folks that prosperous don't usually pick up and move. Mostly, movers are poor folks."

Flynn turned around, ignoring Hickman. "Cable was shot in front," he said, "and any man who can get lead into Vin Cable in front is entitled to it, but I'm a curious man."

Briefly, Radigan explained, telling the story simply and without embellishment from the moment he saw the trail across the meadow. Despite himself, Flynn was fascinated. A fighting man himself he read between the lines. Most men would have gotten themselves killed in such a situation, but Radigan had outthought, out-tricked and outshot his man.

"He have a grudge against you?"

"I never knew who he was until Hickman put a name to him." Radigan paused. "Jim, I'd suggest you examine their papers before there's any trouble. They'll have some sort of a trumped-up claim, I'm sure of that. But look them over."

"Papers?"

"They'll have a deed or something. They wouldn't just come in here and demand a ranch without something to show."

Jim Flynn felt like a fool. He had been ready to order a man off his ranch on the mere say-so of a bunch of strangers. He must see those papers . . . worst of it was, he had a time with reading. He felt irritated and trapped. When he had taken this job it had promised peace and quiet with only an occasional drunken Indian to make trouble—and now this.

When Radigan rode his horse into the ranch yard John Child came out of the house with a lantern. He watched Radigan dismount stiffly and within the warm stable he listened while Radigan stripped bridle and saddle and related the events of the afternoon.

"It's a hard-case outfit," he said finally, "and my hunch is the man behind it is that Harvey Thorpe, the girl's foster brother. He did little talking, but he did a lot of looking and listening."

"And they're bringing cattle? If they get caught in

the canyon by a heavy fall of snow they won't have any more cattle than a jaybird."

"That's working for us . . . they don't know this country. I started small and built carefully and most of the stock we have now was born right here, and they've learned to rustle for their grass in rough country."

The R-Bar was almost twenty-eight miles north of San Ysidro. There were two Indian villages closer, and a few white men in each, but none that concerned him. In the time he had lived on Vache Creek there had been few visitors, and most of them riders passing through, and not one that he could place as a possible scout for the Foley outfit. Most of the riders, and he could count them on the fingers of his hands, had been drifters heading for the breaks to the north to hide out from the law, heading for Loma Coyote.

Did Angelina Foley know of what this range consisted? The rugged mountains, high mesas, hidden valleys and hanging meadows? His cattle were scattered because of the grass, and now were mostly held in proximity to stacks of cut hay, yet here and there he had built fences, utilizing natural features of the terrain wherever possible. During that first winter he had been constantly in the saddle, scouting the places where the wind left grass exposed and where snow did not drift. Coming from Illinois he had known something of cold weather before he came west, and during the drifting years he learned more both from his own experiences and from ranchers he talked to in Montana and Nebraska. It would require such knowledge for these newcomers to survive.

Child shivered. The wind off the mesa was cold, this time of night. "If you need hands," he suggested, "there's some you could have."

"Look, John," Radigan said, "if this comes to a shooting fight, you don't have to stay. It's my fight, and—"

"Oh, shut up! You can't hold this down alone and you damn' well know it. Nor would I let you if you could."

He led the way to the house. "How much do they claim?"

"Twenty-two sections. Take 'em four or five years to find it all."

"How much do you claim? I don't recall you ever told me."

"Don't recall you asking. I claim about twice that much, and I need every bit of it. I was figuring on selling out next year and keeping only the young stuff. I want to build to five or six thousand head."

"You'll need grass."

"I know where it is, lots of it."

Inside the house, Radigan glanced around with surprise. The place had been cleaned thoroughly, the floors scrubbed, the windows washed, and all the pots were shining. "You expecting visitors, John?"

Child shrugged, his face bland. "No tellin' when a bachelor goes to town. Time you were married, anyway."

"Me?" Radigan was astonished. "Now where would you get an idea like that? And where would I find a girl who would have me? I wouldn't know how to treat her unless she had horns."

Radigan went prowling for bear sign and found a dishpan piled high with them. "You stay out of them," Child admonished. "Spoil your supper."

"Seems to me," Radigan said, "you're the one who should get married. You're getting fussier all the time. Should have married years ago."

Child surprised him. "I was married, one time. Married a Cheyenne girl I stole from the Utes who'd taken her prisoner one day. She was right pretty, and mighty scared of those Utes, so I spoke her language and it was a comfort to her. Nighttime I cut loose a couple of horses and the girl and took out. They chased me more'n a hundred miles."

"What happened?"

"We lived north of here. Had one boy, but he was killed in a fall from a horse. Utes again. We were travelin' when they came up on us. They got my wife, shot her through the head first off. I made a run for it with the boy, and he was killed, too."

"Tough."

"We had some good years . . . raised a girl, too. She lived with us four, five years and then we put her in a convent in Mexico. She was thirteen then."

"She wasn't your daughter?"

"No. Comanches took her from a wagon train where they'd killed her family. I traded four horses for her. She stayed at that convent a couple of years, then she lived with some highclass Mexican woman and her husband until they decided to go to Spain. She didn't want to go."

Radigan filled his plate and sat down at the table. He had not realized he was so tired. Part of it was the warm room after the long, cold ride—he felt sleepy.

"Whatever happened to her?"

Child cleared his throat and Radigan glanced at him. "What's the matter?" Radigan demanded. "Are you sick?"

"No. Well—she's coming here."

"*What?*" Radigan was wide awake. "Are you crazy? What would we do with a girl here in the middle of a fight?"

"Where else can she go? And when I told her to come on, well, this here fight wasn't heard of. She's eighteen now and she figures I'm the only person she can come to."

Radigan got to his feet, exasperated and worried. "Damn it, John! What's got into you? This is no place for a girl. Why, she's not even a blood relative!"

"Seems like she is. Wrote to me all the time. She always wanted to come back to the mountains. I guess I was the only father she ever had, although I ain't fixed to be much of a father. She always wanted to come back here, but I talked her into staying on. Those were mighty fine folks she was with and I figured a girl should learn about things like keepin' a fine house and such."

Radigan was exasperated. There was no use blaming John Child, but to have a girl coming here at this time . . . if one thing was needed to make matters worse, this was it. Two men can go on the dodge in the hills no matter what the weather, but they'd have trouble enough caring for themselves without carting a female along.

"Seems I might take her to Santa Fe," Child admitted reluctantly, "but she wanted to be with me, and well, she never really had a father."

Radigan looked at him, then his good humor got the better of him and he laughed. "This is worse than the fight. That we could get out of. What do we know about women?"

When supper was over he went outside, first lowering the light, to make a final round of the ranch. The news meant that John Child must go and he would have to stay on alone. With only two men it would be bad enough, but one man alone?

Not for an instant did he consider allowing the girl to remain. It was no place for even an Indian girl to be, let alone a girl who had grown up in a convent. The house was a position that could not be held throughout a long fight. If they could make a brief stand there it would be fortunate, but they must plan to get away, to move, to keep themselves alive.

The object of battle was the destruction of the enemy's capacity to resist. And as long as they were mobile they were free and able to fight back. If they were tied down they would be destroyed.

The principle of warfare, so far as Tom Radigan was concerned, was attack, always attack. It did not matter that he would be alone, or outnumbered at best, he must attack. Even a stronger enemy could be put on the defensive and kept there.

This was the reason behind the secret caches of food and ammunition, and every move was being made with the idea of retreat to the forest and mountains. And tomorrow they would begin pushing stock back farther into the remote valleys.

Two days they worked, and it was hard, driving work

from morning until night, with the late hours before bedtime devoted to planning. And then Jim Flynn showed up.

"They've got the papers," he said. "They've got a deed. It was a grant from Governor Armijo giving them title to the old Villasur grant."

"He didn't have it to give. That grant isn't worth the paper it's written on, Jim."

"I don't know about that, but you've got to get off."

"No court has ordered me off. My title hasn't been disputed in court. These people are trying to run a bluff. Armijo didn't own that land, the state didn't own it. He had no title to give anyone, and believe me it will take a lot more than they have to get me off."

"We've got to settle this thing," Flynn protested irritably. "I won't have a cattle war."

"Then please remember I'm in possession. Let them go to court. That's the proper way to advance a claim, not by hiring a gunman and trying to kill the man in possession."

"You don't know they did that."

"Who else?" Radigan turned toward the door. "Come on in, Jim. Let's talk about this. Anyway," he added, "what are they going to do if I don't move? Use force? You talk to them, Jim. Believe me, they haven't a leg to stand on."

Flynn sat his saddle stubbornly. He could not believe that such people as Angelina Foley and Harvey Thorpe would try to push a claim to which they had no legal right. He was sure that Radigan was wrong and his persistence was irritating. Never had he had any business with land titles or courts. His experience with the law was simply the enforcement of it against toughs and gunmen.

Radigan turned around. "Jim, tell them to take their claim to court. I'm staying on."

"You're almighty sure," Flynn said angrily. "What are you—a lawyer?"

Radigan walked back to the horse. "Jim, between 1825 and 1828 there were three temporary governors here in New Mexico, and one of them was Armijo. In 1837 there was a rebellion at Taos and a mob of rebels killed Governor Perez. Armijo managed to become commander of the counterattack and when it was successful had himself proclaimed governor.

"There's a lot of stories and at this late date a man can't get at the truth of it all, but there's folks that say he murdered a lot of people including the rebel governor as well as some of his own supporters and friends. He managed to bribe himself into favor with the government of Mexico and his appointment was confirmed.

"He was replaced in 1844 by Lejana, but after a year he was back in office, and making a mint of money by holding up traders on the Sante Fe Trail for a heavy tax on each wagon.

"Moreover, he finagled around with some of the old land grants and rewarded friends with grants of land to which he had no legal title. My guess is that this Foley girl got hold of one of those old grants and she's trying to make it work for her."

Flynn was out of his depth and knew it. He could handle a drunk or a lynch mob, and on two occasions had shot it out with gunmen who wanted to prove themselves. The only legal paper he knew anything about was a warrant.

"You got as much?" Flynn demanded belligerently. "What's your claim? Squatter's rights?"

Radigan shook his head patiently. "Jim, I have legal title to all the land I need, including water rights, and more than that, I'm in possession. My title will stand investigation. These people are deliberately trying to put me off land that I own."

"Don't blame me!" Flynn said angrily. "Don't blame me if the lid blows off!"

Tom Radigan put his big hands on his hips. "I won't blame you, Jim, but I suggest you go to them and order them to stay out of this part of the country. You're the deputy sheriff, and these people will be breaking the law."

Flynn's face darkened. "You don't tell me my job! I know my job, and I'll do it!"

"You seem ready to enforce the law against me," Radigan replied. "And I'm the only one who is in the clear."

"I ain't so sure about that!" Flynn swung his horse. Without a backward glance he started down the trail toward town. It was going to be a long, dark ride.

Two miles below the ranch and overlooking the canyon of Vache Creek was a huge promontory that thrust itself out from the canyon wall like a great watch tower, and there Tom Radigan took up his post. By day a man could see for miles down the canyon, and by night he could hear. The still, cold air let sound travel for miles.

Leaving his horse picketed near a clump of aspen he walked out on the broad brow of the promontory and seated himself beside a rough wall of stone that gave partial shelter from the cold wind.

There were other trails. One led over the Nacimientos behind him from the Rio Puerco, but it was a dim trail known to few besides the Indians and difficult to follow. There was another from the east that led from the Springs to Cebolla and then the mesa to a point just opposite his present position. The chance that they would know of either of the trails was slight.

At midnight he turned over the watch to John Child and at daybreak, after a quick breakfast, he was in the saddle. "She should be there," Child told him. "The way I figure she should be coming in on today's stage, but you'd be better off to let me go. I d'clare, Tom, sometimes I don't figure you're in your right mind . . . they don't even know me."

"They'd know. They'd have you spotted in no time. The risk is mine, so you just sit tight and be sure nobody moves in while I'm gone."

"Tom," Child hesitated, "want I should ride up to Loma Coyote? Or I could send up a smoke? There's some good men up there, fighting men."

"Forget it." Radigan started his horse and then

looked back. "If you see any of them, find out who's around."

"Stark is there." Child walked after the horse. "You remember Adam Stark. He was a Ranger the same time you were, killed a man in El Paso and went up the trail. Best rifle shot I ever saw."

"Good man."

San Ysidro was quiet under the late autumn sun. It was just short of noon when he rode the buckskin down the street and almost the first man he saw was Sam Coker. They tied up at the rail only a few feet apart, but Radigan was not worried. Coker was a trouble hunter, but it was rare that a trouble hunter would start something without an audience.

Hickman was seated at a table in his soiled buckskins, his feet on the table and a bottle at hand. Hickman, Radigan had noticed, always had a bottle but the level of it rarely diminished.

The room was long and low, the building was adobe. The bar was half its length, and there were only a few tables, it was a shabby, down-at-heel room bare of any decoration aside from the fly-specked mirror behind the bar. Downey was at once the stage agent and saloonkeeper, a lonely, hard-faced man who had tended bar in a dozen boom mining towns and who retained few illusions.

"Stage be in about one o'clock?" Radigan asked.

"Should be." Downey pushed a bottle at him. Downey liked him, Radigan believed, as much as he liked any man, but he must be getting a lot of business from the newcomers.

"Join me?" Hickman suggested, pulling his feet off the table. He glanced past Radigan at Sam Coker who had come up to the bar.

Radigan carried his own bottle to the table. "The sign doesn't read for peace," he commented.

Hickman grinned. "I can read the smoke." The door had opened and two other men came in. "The big one is Barbeau. He fancies himself in a brawl. He picked a fight with a drifter the other night and gave him a wicked beatin'. The other one is Bitner."

Downey brought them a tray of food and Barbeau turned to watch. "And the condemned man ate a hearty meal," he said.

"And Balaam's ass spoke," Radigan said.

Barbeau turned sharply around and stared at him, while Downey chuckled and Hickman grinned widely. Two other men at another table were both grinning.

"What was that?" Barbeau asked.

But the moment had passed, and Radigan was eating, ignoring him. Barbeau stared at him, then looked around truculently, hoping for some false move. He was ignored and after a minute he turned his attention again to Radigan. "I wonder if he can fight like he can eat," he asked.

"Maybe somebody should find out," Coker suggested.

Radigan was enjoying the meal, as he had not realized how hungry he was. "Hadn't figured I was this hungry," he said, "but John made some bear sign the other day and I've eaten nothing else for the last two days."

"You want warriors," Hickman said. "You let that get out. You could get more fighting men with bear sign than you could with money, grub being what it is in this country." He filled his glass. "I've seen cowhands ride sixty, seventy mile for chance at bear sign."

Barbeau took another drink and then turned with his back to the bar. He was spoiling for a fight and did not like being ignored, and the drinks had fired his blood and convinced him he was ready.

At the table Radigan had missed nothing. An old campaigner when it came to brawls, he knew every move that was being made. He glimpsed Coker moving a little toward the door to cut off any retreat, and Bitner had moved toward the rear. Barbeau was a broad, thick man with a coarse beard and the thick hands of a really powerful man. He had heavy features and a hard jaw set above a short, thick neck.

Low-voiced, Radigan told Hickman, "Stay out of it. This is my fight."

Hickman studied him quizzically. "Three's quite a handful," he commented. Then he added, "He comes right in, slamming with both hands. And he's hard to stop."

Barbeau was getting set. Radigan needed no map to see how the trail lay, and he sat very still, looking into his cup and mentally cataloguing the room around him and its tactical possibilities. And then the door opened and Angelina Foley came in.

She came directly to Radigan's table and he got to his feet politely.

"Now look at that!" Barbeau sneered. "A real gent!"

"Mr. Radigan?" Her eyes were even greener than he had remembered. "I heard you were in town and hoped to see you before you left. I wanted to tell you how sorry I was that we are putting you off the land. If we could pay you for your trouble . . . ? The offer is still open."

"You're mistaken, Miss Foley. Someone has given you some wrong information again. I'm not moving."

"Please!" Her finger touched his sleeve and her eyes were very large. "We own the land, and you must go. I am afraid that if you do not go some of my men will want to force you to move. I thought . . . well, when I heard you were in town I hoped we might reach an agreement."

"Will you sit down?"

She hesitated an instant, then seated herself. Radigan sat down and as he did so he heard Coker say, "Any minute now, they'll serve tea."

Radigan turned to Downey. "Do you have any tea?"

"Tea? *Tea!* . . . Well . . . sure, but—"

"Make some, and serve it to us here, will you? But make a lot . . . make a gallon of it."

"A *gallon? Of tea?*"

"That's right."

Hickman leaned back in his chair studying Radigan

with a curious glint in his eyes, but Radigan turned to
Angelina. "You were about to say——?"

"I wish you'd reconsider . . . I mean, about moving.
And I meant what I said about paying for your improvements. Naturally, we are as sorry about this as
you."

"But I'm not sorry." Radigan smiled at her. "I'm not
sorry at all. I do regret that you have come so far
without checking, without knowing what you were getting into. If you really wish to see how little you have in
your favor, just take it to court."

"But the courts are so far away, Mr. Radigan!" Her
eyes opened wide. "And they take far too much time!
I am sorry, indeed, but Mr. Thorpe and I have more
than three thousand head of cattle coming up, and if
you won't move, we'll have to move you."

"Know anything about that land, ma'am?"

"I haven't seen it, of course, but Mr. Thorpe has.
Why do you ask?"

"Simply this. If I were to move off that ranch and let
you have it, you couldn't winter three thousand head of
cows up there . . . if you had a free hand and no trouble
at all, you still couldn't do it. There isn't range enough,
there isn't feed enough. If a man had a good winter he
might get through with a thousand head."

She stared at him, taken by his obvious sincerity,
but not wanting to believe him. "But I heard it was the
finest grass in the world, and that there was plenty of
water."

"It is all of that, but there isn't enough of it. I've
hoped to open trails to other valleys where cattle could
be kept, but as it is, that's mostly timber country, over
half of it stands on edge, and probably the easiest way
to be rid of you would be to step out and let you try it.
You'd lose cattle, men and horses."

"You seem to have done all right. I can scarcely
believe you, Mr. Radigan."

He nodded to indicate the men at the bar, aware
they were listening. "Above all, what will you do with
your hands?" It was a chance to inject some doubt into

their minds. "There isn't work up there for more than two or three men on the few acres you'll have."

"Acres?" she protested. "There are miles, twenty-two square miles, to be exact."

Downey came in with the tea. "Had to use two pots," he explained. "Never had such a big order before."

Radigan took the smallest pot and filled their two cups and then he quietly drew his gun. "Serve the rest of it to them." Radigan indicated the three men at the bar with his gun barrel. "I'll see that they drink it."

Coker's features stiffened and his hand started for his gun but stopped as Radigan's gun muzzle swung to cover him. "Start drinking. You, too, Barbeau."

"I'll be damned if I do!"

Radigan's gun tilted a little. "You asked for a tea party and now you've got it. Start drinking or I start shooting."

Hickman was grinning widely. Startled, Angelina Foley could only stare from Radigan to her men, astonished and unbelieving.

"If you aren't drinking by the time I count three," Radigan said casually, "I'll break an arm for each of you."

He came easily to his feet and moved across the floor toward them, keeping Angelina and the door in his line of vision.

"I'll kill you for this!" Barbeau shouted.

"Maybe—but I can start shortening the odds right here. You wanted tea, now get on with it."

Coker slammed down his cup. "I'll be damned if I will!" he shouted and grabbed at his gun butt.

Radigan's gun barrel slashed right and left and Coker hit the floor as if dropped from a roof. "Get on with the tea drinking," Radigan said calmly, "or I'll pile you three deep."

Angelina Foley was white with anger. "See here!" she protested. "You can't do that!"

"I'd hate to hit a woman," he said.

Involuntarily, she sat down. "You . . . you wouldn't dare!"

"If you play games with men," he replied, "you'll play by men's rules."

He handed his six-gun to Hickman. "Barbeau was hunting a fight," he said. "You just keep them off my back."

Barbeau slammed down his cup and turned sharply around. "Fight?" he yelled. "You'd fight *me?*"

Radigan hit him.

Barbeau staggered and Radigan stepped in, watching Barbeau's fists, and whipped a wicked left into Barbeau's belly. Barbeau was a talker as well as a fighter—he had expected to do some talking about what he was going to do, and he had been startled by Radigan's willingness to fight, and the savagery of Radigan's attack confused him. He backed away, but Radigan gave him no chance to get set. A left and right to the face shook him up, and desperately he put his head down and charged, swinging.

A wild right staggered Radigan, but the rancher stepped outside of a left and brought his fist down on Barbeau's kidney. The heavier man gasped and plunged in, grabbing for a clinch. Radigan hit him flush on the chin with a short right that stopped him in his tracks.

Barbeau stared through his raised fists at Radigan. This fight was not going as his fights usually went. The right he had taken was a stunning blow, and Radigan looked cool and easy, not even breathing hard. For the first time Barbeau realized he might be whipped and the thought was maddening. Recklessly he charged, swinging powerful blows with both hands. For a few minutes they fought hard, and Barbeau drove Radigan back across the room. Bitner was cheering, and Barbeau was sure he had Radigan going. He felt his right land solidly, and automatically he slowed to let Radigan fall.

In the instant he slowed, Radigan struck him in the mouth, splitting his lip and spilling blood over his shirt front. Astonished, Barbeau saw Radigan standing befor him . . . the rancher had taken his best punch and had struck back at almost the same instant.

Barbeau rushed, but the heart was out of him. Wildly, he knew he was not going to win. Never before had he hit a man solidly with his right hand when that man had not fallen, but the punch apparently had left Radigan undisturbed. Radigan had grown up around the camps of Michigan loggers before coming west to Texas, and he had served a postgraduate course in fist-fighting among the freighters and the riverboatmen. Few cowhands of the seventies knew anything about fist-fighting. Arguments were settled with guns and fists rarely used, hence Barbeau's victories had been won over men to whom fist-fighting was completely foreign. To Radigan fist- and skull-fighting had been a way of life from boyhood into young manhood. He had lost fights, but he had won many more, and Barbeau had none of the rough skill to which he was accustomed.

Barbeau rushed again, trying to grapple with Radigan, but the rancher gave ground suddenly and the overbalanced Barbeau fell forward. Grabbing Barbeau by the collar, Radigan jerked him forward over his own extended leg and hurled him to the floor.

Barbeau lay on his back, staring up at Radigan from dull eyes.

Then slowly he started to get up, and Radigan backed off to give him room. When Barbeau was on his feet, Radigan walked in, feinted, and hit the heavier man in the belly. Filled with tea, Barbeau backed up, gasping and gulping, overcome with nausea. He backed away, lifting a hand to ward Radigan off. He was battered, bloody and beaten, and he knew it.

Radigan picked up his gun and dropped it into his holster. Coker was sitting on the floor holding his head in both hands.

"I don't want trouble," Radigan said, "but I won't run from it."

He turned to face Angelina Foley. Her face was white, her eyes hard with anger.

"I doubt if you realize what that Vache Creek country is like," he said, "but if you want to come up with one man, and I'd suggest Ross Wall, who is a cowman,

I'll show it to you. Most of it is over seventy-five hundred feet above sea level, and it is the most beautiful mountain country in the world. It is also one of the roughest, coldest and has the most snow."

Downey was standing near the window. "Stage coming," he said.

Radigan put on his hat and walked outside. His knuckles were split and sore but he felt good. It had been his first fist fight in a long time, and he was suddenly glad he had put in much of the summer splitting rails for fences and cutting wood for winter. Nothing like an ax or a crosscut saw to put a man in shape.

He remembered Thorpe. With him such a fight might be different, for Thorpe was no Barbeau, and despite the fact that he looked the fashionable young man there were shoulders on him, and there was something about the lean savagery of his face that was a warning. Also, when they had first met he had noticed scars on the man's knuckles.

The door closed behind him and he turned to see Angelina Foley looking at him. Her gaze was cool, curious, and, for the first time, almost respectful. "Would you have struck me?" she asked curiously.

He had never struck a woman in his life, but he looked at her as if surprised by the question. "Why, of course," he said. "I meant what I said."

"You're no gentleman, Mr. Radigan!"

He grinned at her. "No gentleman would have a chance, dealing with you. You'd tease, flatter, maybe cry. You'd pet him, lie to him, cheat him. Well, you can cry for me or pet me, but you'll never do the rest. Try cheating me and I'll spank your little bustle."

Her eyes held a challenge. "We may be on opposite sides, but you're a man, and I like you. You may call me Gelina."

"You're a beautiful, desirable woman," he said, "but I wouldn't trust you across the street. Before this is over you'll hate me more than you ever hated any man, but seriously, take my advice and leave now. This fight will exhaust everything you've got and leave you nothing."

She smiled. "You have one man working for you, Mr. Radigan. I have thirty. I think I'll win."

He nodded seriously. "But I have something else working for me. The most dangerous ally a man could have—the weather. What will you do with your cattle when the ground is three to six feet deep in snow and no feed anywhere?"

The stage rolled to a stop and the cloud of dust that had pursued it now caught up and drifted over it, settling on the horses and around them.

Radigan watched the driver climb stiffly down from the box, his face red from the chill wind. Hickman had followed him out, and Downey was opening the door to help the passengers down. Radigan shifted his weight and a board creaked under his feet. Looking across the stage he gazed toward the distant mountains, and then a girl got out of the stage and the easy banter stopped as if cut with a knife. Whatever Tom Radigan had expected it was not this.

Under a perky little bonnet her eyes were guileless and blue, her face was that of an innocent child but her body was such that no clothing could conceal the lines of her figure. He caught his breath, half-hypnotized as she came up the steps. He was aware that everyone on the walk was staring, and aware she was thoroughly enjoying it.

She turned to Downey and said, "I am looking for Mr. Child or Mr. Radigan, of the R-Bar."

Downey started to speak but his lips found no words. In this land of few women there was nothing in his experience that prepared him to cope with this emergency. He stared and his lips parted and then he dumbly indicated Radigan.

She turned to him and surveyed him gravely out of large blue eyes. "You're not my father," she said, "so you must be Mr. Radigan."

Her eyes went past him to Gelina Foley. "Is this your wife?"

Radigan chuckled. "No, ma'am, this is my enemy, Miss Gelina Foley."

She looked at Gelina with a thoughtful expression. "I think she's my enemy," she said. "She likes you."

Hastily, Radigan said, "Gretchen—that is your name isn't it?—can you ride?"

"I can ride anything that wears hair," she said, "but I'll have to change my dress." She glanced quickly at Gelina. "Do you like her?" she whispered audibly.

Gelina's face flushed and deliberately she gathered her skirt and descended to her buckboard where Bitner was waiting to help her in. Without a backward glance, they drove away. Inwardly she was fuming. Why! That . . . that baggage!

Angrily, Gelina flounced in her seat. The very idea! Why, that girl was no more than a child! And with a body like that! Accustomed to the attention of men, she realized jealously that from the moment that girl had gotten out of the stage nobody had so much as looked at her.

Her anger, she realized, was unreasonable. She sat back in the buckboard and began to plan. They must move at once, and she would run them out of the country. They would not wait any longer. After all, there were but two men there, and they could not be on watch all the time and still do the things that had to be done.

Her brows gathered. He had spoken of snow. Involuntarily she glanced at the dull sky. But that was nonsense. It never grew very cold here, this was New Mexico. Nonetheless the leaden sky depressed her, and without knowing why she was increasingly worried. Remembering what Radigan had said, she began to wonder just what it was Harvey Thorpe had in mind— it was he who had insisted they come here. But leaving Texas was imperative, and this was the only property to which they had claim. And it should take only a few days to be rid of Radigan.

Yet even as she thought that she remembered the cool, masterful, almost easy way in which he had beaten Barbeau. She had rarely seen a man whipped more thoroughly. And Vin Cable was dead—there had been four bullet holes in his body.

It was not going to be as easy as Harvey believed. Suddenly, she was glad Ross was along.

Gretchen Child returned from Downey's home where she had met Mrs. Downey, a buxom, motherly Irish woman, and where she changed her clothes. She now wore a neat gray riding habit and whatever the dress had left to imagination the habit revealed. Uncomfortably, Radigan was aware that she would be unlikely to find anything that would make her look less exciting than she was.

As if, he reflected grimly, the Thorpe-Foley trouble was not enough!

He helped her into the saddle but she really needed no help. He saw at a glance that whatever else she might be she was at home in a saddle.

"You'll not be able to stay at the ranch," he warned. "It won't be safe."

"I trust you," she said.

Hastily, he explained. "I didn't mean that. We've a range war on with those people back there. A shooting war, I think."

"I saw your knuckles. Has the war started?" She looked at him seriously. "I'm strong. I can work, and I can use a gun. I'm really strong." She held out her arm, doubled to make a muscle. "Just feel of that."

three

The cattle came first. They came up the canyon on the third day after Radigan's return with Gretchen Child, and they came in a solid mass, hurried on by a dozen cowhands. Obviously they had been driven up the canyon earlier and held at the *cienaga* during the night.

The cattle came first and they came fast. Radigan was putting a little feed in the makeshift corral hidden among the fallen rocks from the weathering of the mesa when he heard Child yell.

He heard him yell, heard a shot, and he dropped the pitchfork and came running. He shot the first steer into the yard, but a glance told him there was no stemming that tide of beef and he ducked into the house after John and slammed the door, dropping the bar into place. Almost before he could reach the window the yard was crowded with cattle.

Child rested the muzzle of his Winchester on the sill of the window beyond the door and glanced over at Radigan. "Smart," he said, "mighty smart. We're not supposed to get out."

A big steer was pressed tight against the door, and others were so close to the windows that Radigan could have reached out and scratched their backs. The ranch yard was jammed full of steers pressed in a compact mass. Beyond them, to left and right, the herd was spreading out in loose formation, but those in the yard were held tight by a circle of cowhands and tight-drawn ropes. The cowhands were out of sight behind the barn or in other concealment.

"Hi, the house!" The voice was the booming one of Ross Wall. "You want to get out, toss your guns out the window!"

Child glanced at Radigan but he motioned for silence. Several minutes passed. After the first few minutes of realization Gretchen had calmly returned to her housework, putting a meal on the table as though there was no enemy within miles. Yet Radigan noted she wore riding boots and a rough skirt—she was ready to go.

Wall did not know about the tunnel, and that was what would save them. Nobody knew about that but John Child, and obviously somebody in town had told Wall or Thorpe or both of the fact that the ranch house had but one entrance.

And without the tunnel they would have been helpless, for there was no escape from the house except by the tunnel, for driving the beef into the yard had imprisoned them just as surely as if walled with stone. They could kill the beef, but if they did they would then be killed themselves and no one would say they were killed without cause.

"If you want to eat," Gretchen said, "it's ready."

"Go ahead, John. You sit down. I'll take mine here at the window."

"Hello, the house!" It was Wall again. "Radigan, I know you're in there, and you haven't a prayer! Throw us your guns and we'll let you out!"

They would get the house, but at this time of year, hoping to move in themselves, they would not burn it. Living in the hills would be rough but they could stand it for a short time, at least. Keeping well back away from the window, Radigan considered the situation.

Long ago he had planned for just such an emergency, but he had expected the trouble from the Utes. He had built for defense, but had planned for abandoning the place if it became necessary. Here, as at the barn, there was another way out, but the way out of the house was through a tunnel that opened in thick brush at the foot of the mesa near where the horses were picketed. It was not far behind the house, and it was unlikely anyone would examine the talus slope at the mesa's foot. To the casual eye it looked like a thousand other such slopes at the base of a thousand such mesas.

There was no way they could get at the house from the rear so it was unlikely anyone would find reason for checking that slope.

He could hear the murmur of voices from beyond the cattle. Obviously, the fact that no reply came from the house was disturbing to them, for there is no bargaining with a man who won't talk.

Gretchen brought coffee to the window, keeping well out of line. Radigan smiled at her. "You walked right into trouble. I'm sorry."

"Will we have to leave here?"

"Yes."

"We will need blankets and warm clothes," she said. "I'll get them ready."

He watched her as she walked away, amazed anew at the calm with which she accepted the situation. He glanced out the window again . . . they had to stall until after dark, for the chance of escape in daylight was less . . . all was quiet. The cattle were jammed tight and held there, pressing against the door.

Ross Wall hunkered down beside the fire, spreading his cold hands to the flames. "He's there, all right. No way he could get out. I talked to a man down to San Ysidro, man helped build this place and he swears there was only one door. Small house like that, there's no need for another."

Thorpe squatted beside the fire and rolled a cigarette. "We've got to get him out of there. If he's got grub he could spend the winter there."

Wall looked around gloomily. "He sure didn't tell no lies about grass. If this is all there is we can't hold the herd on it for a week."

"There's more."

Wall hunched his heavy shoulders under his coat. The more he saw of the situation the less he liked it, and from all he could see the ranch looked like a two-man operation, and if it started to snow. . . .

"I better start some of the men scouting for grass.

If we don't find some we'll have to drive out of here."

"Are you questioning my judgment?"

Ross Wall rolled his quid in his big jaws. "You said the grass was here, an' Miss Foley took your word for it. I hope you're right."

"It's here."

Harvey Thorpe looked around slowly. The open space before the mesa did not look as large now as it had when empty of cattle, and despite himself he was worried. There was other grass back in the hills, but where was it? He had expected to find well-marked trails and he could find no trails at all. From the appearance of things this was all there was to the R-Bar, yet people at San Ysidro and others at Santa Fe had said Radigan ran several hundred head on land that would support several thousand.

"All right," Thorpe said finally, "send out a couple of men." He studied the house. "There's smoke from the chimney, but it looks like a dying fire."

"Well-built house. They would need little fire."

It was growing colder. Ross Wall looked at the sky. He was a tough, hardheaded man who rode for the brand; an order from Angelina Foley was all he asked from anyone. He was the perfect feudal henchman, and as he had served her father so he now served her, and she was, he thought with satisfaction, a whole lot smarter than her father. Her father would have stayed in Texas and fought it out when there wasn't a chance of winning, but Angelina knew when to cut and run, and what to take with her when she did. They had rustled her herds so when she left she simply drove off everything in sight.

Personally, he thought Radigan correct in his suggestion to sell off the cattle, especially the doctored brands, of which there were too many for comfort. Holding the herd was probably Thorpe's idea, but a man did not always know where the ideas originated for Angelina had a way of attributing ideas that were actually hers to someone else.

He poked a stick into the fire. There was not much

time. They had to get Radigan out of there, but without a killing if possible. Ross Wall held no objections to killing when every other way had been tried, or when necessity demanded, but killings had a way of stirring things up, and a man like Radigan might have many friends.

He had not seen the beating Radigan had given Barbeau, but he had seen Barbeau afterwards and from all accounts it had been a thorough and artistic job, and it had left Barbeau a silent, hard-working man with all the bully knocked out of him for the time. Nothing he had seen of Radigan allowed him to believe that moving the man would be a simple task. He did not believe with Coker that one fast, hard-shooting rush would do it—the man inside that house was intelligent and a fighter.

Wall had been impressed with Radigan's manner—he did not seem to believe himself outnumbered, nor did he hesitate to handle a fight when it came to him. A hard man and a fighter himself, Wall recognized the same traits in his antagonist and respected them. Nonetheless, he had a job to do and the look of the sky bothered him.

Born in Vermont he had come west as a child, but there lingered a memory of mornings at home when his father would come in from the barn coated with snow, and when long icicles hung from the eaves. Those winters had been cold, with a deep, penetrating cold, and men had been frozen to death in some of those winters. This was New Mexico, and he had always thought of it as a warm and pleasant place, which it was, but they were high now and the chill in the air worried him.

Everything either Thorpe or Angelina had was tied up in that herd. Behind there was nothing but enmity and shambles, and the rustled cattle forbade their ever returning to Texas. Their only chance for survival lay right there, digging in fast. Yet he wished they would sell the herd and not gamble.

He looked down at the thick, hard-knuckled hands he held over the fire. He was forty now, no youngster

by Plains standards, and he had worked twenty years
for the Foley outfit. The Old Man had been a pirate,
but a genial one, and in a period of ranching and free
branding he had become rich, but he made enemies
along the way, and tried to take in more territory than
he'd a right to.

Angelina was smarter than her father, and cooler.
When he thought about Angelina, Ross Wall worried.
She was too cold, too shrewd, and she used her beauty
as some men use a gun. Harvey Thorpe now . . . Ross
had never made up his mind about Harvey. The Old
Man married Harvey's aunt and Harvey had always
lived with her, and for a few years Harvey had been the
Old Man's shadow. Then he drifted away, and not
much was known about those years, but when he returned he played a smart hand of poker, and he could
use a gun, and once, when Ross happened on Harvey
when he was changing his shirt, Ross saw bullet scars
on his side—but Harvey had said nothing about them.

The feud broke and the Old Man was killed. Harvey
had acted fast. Ross never knew exactly what happened
but the man that killed the Old Man was shot to death
at close range in his own doorway, and when his son
ran around the house, Harvey had killed him, too.

The fighting had been sporadic for several years, but
the men Harvey gathered around him were fighters
rather than punchers and the ranch deteriorated while
attention was given to fighting a feud they could not
win, and along with it came lawless acts perpetrated by
some of the men Harvey brought in. There came a time
when it had ceased to be a feud with other families and
had become a community matter, and word came to the
ranch that vigilantes were being organized by the solid
people of the community to act if the Rangers failed—
and they had been sent for.

Flight followed, and a wholesale sweep of all the cattle they encountered in moving. Ross liked none of it,
but about some of those cattle there was a question of
title so he had gone along. And now they were here,

and inside that house was a tough man who had to be dislodged and they could not burn him out.

He drew back his warmed hands and rolled a smoke. All through the Texas trouble he had left the fighting to Thorpe and had worked to preserve the ranch, without hands enough and without money enough. While gunhands loitered about the ranch or swaggered it in saloons, the water holes were trampled into mud, cattle died bogged down in swamps and fences torn down that allowed cattle to stray into the breaks when not actually rustled.

Of the hands he now had only six or seven were good punchers. The others were fighting men, gunhands like Barbeau and Coker or men he suspected of cold-blooded murder like Leach.

One thing Radigan said had stuck in his mind. The remark had been passed on to him by one of the hands. By Bitner, in fact. Radigan had said cattle could be handled on this range with few men: if that were so he might get rid of this lot they now had. Huddled near the fire, he considered that, and wondered how far he might go without trouble with Thorpe, for it was he who wanted such men about. He wanted to be rid of Coker, most of all. And after him, that troublemaker Barbeau who had driven two of his best hands to quit.

Ross Wall got to his feet. "Going to look around," he said, to no one in particular.

Thorpe did not even look up as Wall walked away, but in his mind Wall was thinking of something that had just come to him. He could be rid of Coker, and be rid of him without trouble with Thorpe. The men inside that house were good men with guns, and if Coker happened to get into an exposed position when the shooting started. . . .

Angelina Foley came up the canyon at daybreak in the buckboard and left her rig at the foot of the promontory. From there she rode on up the trail on a horse provided by Wall. The cattle were still jammed tight against the door and the chimney trailed a smoke into the still morning sky. Both Wall and Thorpe sat beside her and looked at the bunched cattle. Few of them had been able to reach water or grass and they were bawling and restless.

She shivered in the early morning air and looked enviously at the trail of smoke coming from the warm, well-built house. Then she turned her eyes from the house and surveyed the area with puzzled eyes. "Harvey," she said, "you told me there was grass here, grass for thousands of cattle."

"He's got several hundred head somewhere," Thorpe replied. "There are valleys around. We'll find them."

"Have you looked?"

"No luck so far," Wall told her. "I've had two men scouting the country but so far not even a trail has turned up."

She looked at the house. "Can't we get them out of there?"

"We can," Wall said reluctantly, "but we'd have to kill Radigan. Might stir up more trouble than we want."

"Those cattle need water," she told them. "Drive them off. I'm going up to the house."

From inside the house Radigan watched the riders come down and watched them move the cattle away. When they were gone, Angelina Foley started for the house. Cautiously, Radigan opened the door. "Always nice to have guests," he said, "get down and come in."

As she entered the door Ross Wall and Thorpe started forward, and Radigan put a bullet into the dirt at their horses' feet. "You stay back," he said, loud enough for them to hear, "we don't want to hurt anybody."

He glanced at John Child who moved to the window with his Winchester.

She stopped inside the doorway and glanced around, surprised at the neatness of the small but compact house, the shining copper kettles, the swept floor, and the inside pump, a rarity anywhere in the West of the period. It was a warm, friendly, comfortable house, and for an instant her eyes met those of Gretchen.

This was the girl she had seen arrive on the stage, the

one who had so angered her. She looked like a lovely young girl now in her simple cotton dress, standing beside the wide fireplace.

"Will you sit down?" Gretchen suggested. "The coffee is hot."

Radigan seated her with all the formality of a gentleman at a fashionable dinner, and Gretchen brought a steaming cup of coffee to the table and a plate of doughnuts.

"You live well here," she said to Radigan. "I'm sorry you have to move."

"We like it here," he commented, ignoring her remark, "and we've learned how to live with the country."

"I don't see much grass," she said. "I confess I believed it to be range country."

"You'll find much that you don't expect," he assured her. "I've seen snow to the eaves of this house. Sometimes in the winter we have to open a tunnel to the barn so we can feed the stock."

She was frankly incredulous, but he continued. "It makes me wonder who could convince you that you wanted to live here, or that you could ranch here. I think there is more behind this than appears on the surface."

"The land is mine," she said, "and that is the only reason we came."

"About that," he tried his coffee and put it down hurriedly. It was much too hot. "Your claim is based on an Armijo grant, and he had no authority to grant land to anyone, nor did he ever have title to this land. This was part of an original grant by the King of Spain, ratified later by the government of Mexico, and still later by the government of the United States.

"It was for years considered useless land, too far from anything and of no immediate use, so I moved in, looked it over, and bought out the original grant. You could have learned in Santa Fe that I have legal title to thirty-six sections in this area. Your grant is not and never was worth anything at all, and whatever your father gave for it it has been lost. I am sorry, but those are the facts. In court you would never have a chance."

She was coldly furious but her expression did not change, yet within her there was a sudden emptiness. Had her father never managed one successful thing? And why had Harvey not discovered this? Why had he not known about the scarcity of grazing land? Yet there was no turning back. There was no way back at all. She could sell her herd—yes. But the cattle were a strong argument in her favor, and an outfit moving into a country with a herd automatically garnered some degree of respect. There was no turning back.

She looked up at him and smiled. "I wish we could settle this peacefully, Mr. Radigan, but you may be sure the case will never go to court. It will be settled right here—now."

She had finished her coffee. Abruptly, he got to his feet. "If that is the case, we're wasting time," he replied brusquely. "We've nothing further to discuss. I am giving you one hour to get your cattle and outfit off my land."

Angelina did not move. She lifted her cup and smiled at him, a radiant smile. "I am sorry we are enemies," she said. "I'd hoped we could be friends."

"We can still be friends," Gretchen suggested. "Move your cattle away and find a ranch of your own and then come back and see us."

" 'Us?' " she quoted. "Well!" Angelina got to her feet. "I was not aware that you had become a partner in Mr. Radigan's ranch. "Or," she glanced meaningly from one to the other, "have you already established a claim?"

Gretchen's face grew pale, then flooded with color. "I have no claim," she replied, "only my father is loyal to Tom Radigan and I hope I shall be."

Angelina walked to the door. "You will be," she said. "I have no doubt of it."

She went outside into the cold air and for a minute she stood still, fuming inwardly. That—that little! Then she swung into the saddle. All right then, Harvey knew how to do it. Yet even as her decision was made she kept seeing the way Radigan's dark hair curled around his ears, and the grave thoughtful expression of his eyes.

And soon he would be dead . . . killed.

No matter. He had had his chance. And there was no other way. She kept telling herself that.

Harvey Thorpe hunched his shoulders against the cold, and glanced irritably at the gray sky. "You're sure there isn't another door?"

"I looked. There was only the one."

"What do you think, Ross?"

Wall shifted his weight in the saddle. "We can do it, but we're going to lose men. No use trying it from behind. A man coming off that rock slope would get himself shot to doll rags."

Thorpe looked at the house. They could move into the barn and shoot into the house through the windows, but it wasn't going to be easy. Radigan was apparently set for a siege. "We've got it to do," he said.

"Coker's a good man with a gun," Wall suggested. "If we could get Coker and Barbeau where they could cover the windows, we might make it too hot for them to stay in there."

"All right," Thorpe swung his horse, "let's take it."

Ross Wall moved swiftly. The cattle were driven into the bottoms and held in a loose herd by four men, and the others climbed into position where they could fire upon the house. Three men occupied the barn and two moved into the corrals, and there was no firing. Coker he placed among the trees to the right of the house, Barbeau to the left.

Angelina rode back down the hill and dismounted near the fire. She extended her hands toward the flames, watching Bitner, who had remained by the fire for the time being. "You've seen him. What do you think about him?" she asked.

Bitner glanced at her out of his tough, cynical eyes. "You never seen a cattle war, ma'am," he said. "This here shapes up like a first-rate one. Man never knows

when one starts as to how it will end, or where. Yes,
I've seen him close up, and he ain't no bargain. That
there Radigan is a grizzly bear from way back in the up
hills. He'll take some killin' an' when he dies he won't
go by himself. I hired on for fightin' wages. Ma'am, I
reckon we'll earn 'em."

"There's only two men."

"Two. Ain't many, is it? But they're forted up, an'
they know how to fight." He stirred the fire and piled
on some dried wood. "Two men can make a fight of it,
and that Radigan's a fighter from who flung the chunk."

A rifle shot came to them. It was Coker who had
fired, and they could see the smoke from his position,
although they could not see the house. "Coker," Bitner
said. "He's quick on the shoot."

There was no other sound for several minutes and
Angelina listened the echo away, thinking of what it
might mean. Men might die—but men had died before.
A dozen had died in the feud from which they had just
come, and several more disappeared or wounded.

The shot fired by Coker struck the window sill and
ripped a gash. It was a wooden sill laid on the rock of
the house. Radigan glanced at it and waited. He was in
no hurry. There was no sense shooting until somebody
gave him something to shoot at.

Gretchen, under his orders, was making up three
packs of food. Blankets had already been cached, but
each would take one along and a ground sheet. No telling where all they would camp.

A bullet shattered glass and imbedded itself in the
ceiling. John Child shifted a little, then fired suddenly.
Barbeau jerked back, swearing. There was a burn across
his shoulder that stung like fire and he felt a trickle of
blood down his back. It was only a break in the skin,
but he felt a sudden chill. These men could shoot.

All afternoon there was sporadic fire with no harm
on either side. Harvey Thorpe, nested down among
some boulders, studied the house irritably. Not more
than four shots had come from the house . . . either they
had little ammunition or they were careful. Barbeau had

been scratched, and Coker had a boot heel shot off. Twice shots had come dangerously close to Wall.

The packs were completed and placed near the tunnel door. Child had been out through the tunnel and had fed corn to the hidden horses. He was worried, and stayed with them for some time. Sooner or later somebody was going to try circling behind the house and if they did they would be sure to find the horses. There was little concealment back there, and on much of the talus slope a man would be exposed to fire from below with no cover at all.

When darkness came Radigan slipped outside and waited against the wall of the house with a six-gun. He was sure an attempt would be made to creep under the windows and lie against the wall for quick shots through the windows. He wanted to be ready. Seated with his back against the wall, Radigan waited.

The air was cool, not as cold as it had been, and the dryness seemed gone from the night. A faint wind stirred the pines and out in the stable a horse stomped.

He saw a faint movement near the wall of the barn and the corral corner. And then the man came, bent low and running in his sock feet. Radigan stood up, the darkness of his body merging with the darkness under the wide eaves of the house. The man came up, running quietly, and failed to see Radigan until too late. The gun barrel swept down in an arc and caught the man behind the ear. He slumped, tried to straighten, and Radigan hit him again. He went down then, and lay still. Using some rawhide piggin strings, carried by every cowhand for the purpose of tying a calf's hoofs together after it had been roped and thrown, Radigan tied the man up nicely, and then gagged him with a chunk of old sacking.

The man on the ground groaned, and tried to move. "You take it easy," Radigan advised in a whisper. "It won't do you any good to wear yourself out. You lie still and maybe I won't slug you again."

A slow hour passed, and nothing happened. Then a second man started from the barn, and Radigan saw him coming. He came with a rush, and evidently the prisoner heard him for he grunted loudly and tried to call out. The oncoming man slid to a halt and his gun came up. Radigan dropped to one knee and when the man fired, he replied instantly, and just as quickly, hit the ground and rolled. Over his head bullets thudded and smacked into the house and the bench at the door.

"You try that again," Radigan said to the prisoner, "and you'll get yourself killed by your own outfit."

An hour went slowly by, and Radigan crawled to the door and scratched his signal to come in.

Gretchen was beside him instantly. "Tom, Tom, are you hurt?"

"Just hungry."

"You got one," Child said. "I saw him get it."

"And a prisoner."

Radigan sat at the table and drank coffee in the dark. There was food on the table, and when he had eaten he carried a cup of coffee to the window and drank it while eating a doughnut.

"All right," he said finally. "It's time."

The stars were out when they reached the horses. It took them only a minute or two to saddle up. Child strapped on the packs and they led the horses off the slope into the trees. In the next few minutes they would know if they were going to make it without being discovered.

The trail led close along the mesa and with Child in the lead and Radigan as rear guard, they worked their way along under the trees and away from the house. When they had gone a quarter of a mile they got into their saddles and rode away.

Nobody talked, nor felt like talking. Behind them was the warm comfort of the ranch house and before them lay the forest, the night and the cold. No telling how long it would be before any of them slept under a roof again—if they ever did.

They rode west . . . and there was no trail. They rode west into the somber darkness of the forest, and only occasionally could they see the stars. It was cold . . . a wind from off the high peaks whispered the pines, moved restlessly, making violins of the pine needles, moaning low among the rocks and across the waste spaces above the timberline.

Tom Radigan moved into the lead, for only he knew where they now went, and in the darkness where there was no trail, and where all landmarks had mysteriously disappeared into a common darkness, he led on, knowing his way along the slope of the mountain and finding the openings among the trees as if guided by some mysterious thread.

From behind there came no sound as the besiegers waited for daylight. Two men had advanced to attack, and two men had disappeared, one surely dead and the other vanished. In silence they would be watching the dark house, worried, uncertain, angry.

How long would it be before they knew the house to be empty? Hours, perhaps. And every minute a minute of advantage. In these hills Tom Radigan knew it would take a lot of searching to find him—or an accident. It was like him that he did not discount the possibility of accident.

They might have held out at the house, yet if their horses were discovered there would be no escape at all, and it was always better to be mobile than to be pinned down by the enemy. Yet he did not retreat to escape, he retreated to be able to choose his own time for attack. The battle had been joined now and the time for negotiation was past. Whatever might have been done to avert the fight was now in the past. A man was dead. . . .

An hour they rode, and then they emerged from the trees on a vast slope, dotted here and there with the night black clumps of aspen, and they still rode west with the vast black bulk of the mesa on their right, towering five hundred feet into the sky above them. They rode in silence with only the wind for company and the ragged shadows of sentinel pines for lookouts. Radigan paused once and let the other two ride up beside him.

"How're you coming?" he asked Gretchen.

"All right, Tom. I can ride all night and all day if you like."

"Good girl."

John Child was silent. The moon was up now and the stars faded into its greater light. Only on the horizon were there clouds.

"We're turning north." Radigan pointed west and south with a sweep of his hand. "See that line of mesas? They look like a fleet in battle formation. Well, they point our way north. I think we'll bed down somewhere in the breaks south of Nacimiento Peak."

As the crow flies they had covered no more than three or four miles, although the ground distance was twice that. Now, turning north with the distant, towering peak as guide, they rode again without a trail, riding in single file. Occasionally they were in forest, but much of the distance on long slopes with clumps of aspen and brush.

They traveled slowly for the terrain was unfamiliar even to Child and Radigan. Both men had ridden over it by day, but at night nothing looks the same, and there were no landmarks they remembered. Moreover, their activities had largely centered on the other side of the mountain, east of the ranch. On their left the land fell away in a long slope toward the valley of the Rio Puerco, but this was off the R-Bar range, and out of the territory where their cattle usually strayed.

The night was still. Several times Radigan drew up and listened for any sound of pursuit, but there was no sound but the sound of the wind, always the wind.

Riding along the slope the ground suddenly fell away into a small basin almost filled with a grove of aspen. In the midst of a horseshoe formation of aspen and boulders there was a hollow away from the wind and a faint sound of trickling water. Radigan pulled up. "We'll take a break. Have some coffee."

Child's saddle creaked as he swung down, and Radigan dismounted, reaching a hand up for Gretchen. Her hand was surprisingly strong as she swung down.

"Tired?"

"We've only started."

Despite the rain they found bark from the underside of a deadfall, and leaves in the same place. There were dry branches under the trees, and in a minute or two a small blaze was going. It was very small—a man could cover that fire with his hat—but it was enough for coffee, and small enough to be unseen, sheltered as it was by the low ground and the aspen.

Radigan went back into the darkness and located the spring. An owl went up out of the brush with a *whoosh* of sound and he dropped his hand to his gun, then grinned into the dark. He squatted on his haunches and filled the coffeepot after tasting the water. It was cold and fresh.

Only a trickle, it came out of some rocks and fell into a small basin before trickling off down the slope.

Firelight flickered on the flanks of the horses and reflected from polished saddle leather. Overhead a few stars sparkled, and Tom Radigan squatted on his heels and looked across the fire at Gretchen. There was no sign of weariness in her, and she looked excited and alive. Child caught his eye and grinned. "On the trail again," he said, "I wonder if a man ever gets away from it."

It was cool and damp in the hollow, but the coffee was hot and tasted good. Suddenly he felt exhilarated. All right, so they were in a fight, that Foley outfit weren't getting any virgins if it was fight they wanted. He'd been through the mill and, as for Child, that breed was as tough as they came. He'd been around and over the country, and he'd be in there fighting when that bunch of flat-land punchers were hunting themselves a hole.

Firelight danced with the shadows among the slender trunks of aspen. The leaves pattered daintily in the brief wind, and Radigan huddled his second cup of coffee in his hands and thought about what was coming, but when he thought of that he thought of Angelina

Foley. What was the relationship there? Foster brother? Or something more? And why had they come here?

True, she had a claim on this land, even if one that would hold water in no court, anywhere. But people who are doing well do not often leave the place where they are. She had an outfit of fighting men, and a fore- man who was by all the signs a competent man, if a hard one. So then, why would they leave? An outfit with as many cattle as they had was in no trouble . . . unless they themselves had been driven off their range, or had other trouble.

That might stand some looking into. But none of this need have happened if Deputy Sheriff Flynn had taken a strong stand at the beginning, but now that it had begun there was no telling when it would end. Many such a fight went on for years: like that Sutton-Taylor fight, in Texas; it was not over even now.

When he had carefully put out their fire and smothered any coals remaining he did what could be done to wipe out any evidence of it, placing an old branch over the spot and holding up a handful of leaves to let them fall as they would over the ground below. It would stand no careful check by a tracker, but to the casual eye, if they came this way, it would offer nothing. Mounting up they rode on, pointing toward the dark bulk of Nacimiento Peak. They made camp just after daylight at the fork of Clear Creek back of Eureka Mesa.

They had ridden nearly twenty miles describing a rough half-circle around the ranch area. At their camp they were a mere eight miles from the R-Bar ranch, but the trail they had left would be difficult to follow. For several miles they had ridden across bare rock, and Radigan had used several tricks, such as doubling back on their own trail, following creek beds and the like, and twice he had them separate and make separate trails, later meeting at a chosen rendezvous up ahead.

Their camp was in a rocky gorge where water had hollowed caves from the canyon walls and then had cut lower into the rock leaving the cave levels well above any possible water. In one of these caves, screened by bushes and trees, they made their camp.

"You think they'll trail us? Or just settle down and enjoy themselves?"

"They won't enjoy themselves because we're going back. We're going to see what we can do to make them want to be some place else."

Radigan got up and took his rifle. "I'll take first watch, John. And I'm going to scout around a mite."

It was growing light. Radigan took his Winchester and walked down through the rocks to the mouth of the gorge. Ordinarily he would not have stopped in such a place, but the canyon looked like a good hideout, and there was a chance that before the night was over they would need the shelter the cave afforded. There was also an abundance of driftwood for fuel. And small chance of the place being found. The brush growing before the water-hollowed cave screened it so there could be no reflection on the opposite wall of the canyon. Once away from the cave, it could scarcely be seen. What about up the canyon? He glanced up thoughtfully, but took a way down the canyon to see how much of the country could be seen.

The ranch was about eight miles due south and some of his cattle were not far from here on the Penas Negras. In this area he knew every bit of the country south, and much of it to the east. He remembered again some of the stories he had heard of those canyons to the north. There were outlaws there, and renegade Indians, bronco Utes mostly.

How long would they be stalled before they realized the house was empty? Had they discovered it yet?

He walked down to the mouth of the canyon which ended in a great jumble of boulders, many of them bigger than houses, solid chunks of rock tumbled together in grotesque shapes. And there were cliffs and a thick pine forest.

With his field glass he searched the terrain to the south, studying it with extreme care from the greatest distance to the closest. He picked up several deer, and once a black bear, but nothing human. The view to the west was good, but there, too, he could see nothing.

They would rest for a few hours, and he would make some plans. Despite their long ride they were again within striking distance of the ranch, and he had no intention of allowing the Foley outfit to get settled on the place. Fortunately, the horses he had on pasture were not far from here, held in a small valley that served as a corral with its sheer walls, plentiful grass and water. There were twenty-two head of horses there, most of them wild horses Radigan had himself broken to the saddle. Throughout the early part of the day they loafed and slept, and meanwhile Radigan did some serious thinking. He was a tenacious thinker, who wrestled with an idea until every detail was worked out, and now he realized that with the winter staring them in the face the first thing they needed was a base of operations that was warm, comfortable, and hidden from discovery.

Moreover, he had a few moves to make to render his own position secure. He anticipated no assistance from Flynn, nor would there be any forthcoming from the authorities in Santa Fe, although they would appreciate that right was on his side. But he intended to appeal to both, and to get his case on record. These steps were merely to secure his own position from attack by the law; the counterattacks he would make on his own. He neither expected nor wanted the help of the law.

He finally dropped off to sleep and awakened suddenly to find the canyon filling with shadows. The fire crackled and there was a pleasant aroma of coffee. Gretchen sat by the fire watching him. John Child was still asleep.

Radigan sat up and scratched his head. "Have you slept at all?"

"I'll sleep later. Everything is all right. I took a walk around down the canyon, but there was nothing in sight."

"You'll do to ride the river with," he said. "Did you learn that in a convent?"

"I learned that from Uncle John," she said, indicating Child. "He's as careful as you."

"It's a way of life. And there's times when it is the only way if you want to live." He rolled a smoke and lighted it with a twig from the fire. It was going to be a cold night. "John told me the Indians wiped out your family."

"I remember so little . . . we seemed forever coming west that we lost track of time. At least I did. Sometimes I thought the rumble of wagon wheels was the only sound in the world, that and the wind; there was always the wind in the grass.

"There was my father and mother, and I believe there was an uncle . . . it's so hard to remember. I had gone to the creek after some water with my father, and suddenly we heard shooting and yelling. Oh, I was frightened! Father made me hide in some willows and then he went to see what was happening, and I waited a long time and then went to find him and the Indians saw me."

"They treat you all right?"

"Oh, yes! They were excited about my yellow hair, and they were kind. But they smelled so funny, and I tried not to cry. After that they made me work but they were nice to me and the Indian who found me treated me like his own child."

Radigan walked out into the canyon and, catching a deadfall, dragged it to within easy reach of the cave mouth. It would provide fuel for the night. He walked up the canyon and gathered several large chunks and brought them back to the fire. The rim of San Pedro Mountain was crested with gold from the setting sun, and a deep rose lay along the flank of Nacimiento Peak. The sky was clear.

When he had saddled up he returned to the cave and accepted a cup of coffee. "No time to waste," he said. "I want to get started before the light goes."

"Be careful."

"That I'll be."

He went out to his horse and slid his rifle into the saddle scabbard. Gretchen had followed him out. "Tom —be careful."

A lost ray of sunshine caught her golden hair in a web of gold light.

"Sure," he said, and reining the horse around he cantered down the canyon.

An hour later he was seated on the side of a rugged peak something over a mile from the ranch, studying it with his field glasses. The cattle were standing about, and a horse was tied at the corral. After a moment he saw a man come from the house with a rifle. There was no other movement.

Then when some of the cattle moved he saw the faint flicker of a campfire at the base of the promontory. Several dark figures moved about. Some of the cattle had strayed up almost as far as his own position and he studied them thoughtfully. If a stampede started . . . it was just a thought.

Darkness came suddenly and he came down off the slope and rode down among the cattle. Drifting back and forth across the valley, which was narrow, he started the cattle moving south. He worked slowly and with care, and a cold north wind helped. The cattle turned their tails to the wind and drifted. By the time he was a quarter of a mile from the fire he had at least two hundred head moving south. Suddenly he drew his pistol. For an instant it lay across the pommel of his saddle as he watched the dark figures of the plodding cattle, and then he fired and at the same time let go with a wild Texas yell and spurred his horse into the cattle. They broke and ran with two more shots and his wild yells to urge them on.

More than four hundred head were between his own group and the fire, and they started with a lunge.

There was a wild yell and a shot from the fire and then it was blotted out by a surge of bodies. The stampeding cattle swept over and beyond the fire and went charging off down the canyon. From the house there was a shout and the slam of a door, and then a pound of hoofs. Tom Radigan turned his gelding and walked it across the valley and lost himself against the blackness of the trees.

Skirting the marsh, Radigan found the Cebolla Trail and followed it over the mesa to the cluster of houses that marked the village.

At a house on the edge of town he drew up amid the yapping of dogs and when the house door opened he said, "Pedro, it is Radigan."

The door closed and he heard the pad of bare feet coming toward him. "What is it I can do, señor?"

"That black horse! I'll leave mine here."

"Come!"

Pedro led the way to the corral and roped the black. When the saddle was shifted, Radigan said, "Better hide my horse. These are not good men."

"Do you need help, Señor Tom?"

"No, no help."

"There are men. At Loma Coyote there are men. Good men for the fight. If you wish it I will ride there and they will come to you."

"No, not yet."

He rode south and camped that morning at a spot above San Ysidro. When he had slept an hour the sun was up and he saddled up again and rode down into the town.

Downey was sweeping off the boardwalk in front of the stage station. Slowly, he straightened up. "You're in trouble, Tom," he said. "I heard they ran you off."

"Did you?" Radigan tied the black to the hitching rail and straightened. He needed a bath and a shave, and a good meal. Suddenly he realized how hungry he was. "I left because I didn't want to be pinned down."

Flynn came around the building and stopped when he saw Radigan. The deputy sheriff measured him carefully, and then said, "You leavin' the country?"

"This is my home."

"I'd advise you to leave. You've lost your place,

which means there's nothing to keep you here."

"You've made up your mind then?"

"What d' you mean?"

"You've chosen your side, is that it?"

Flynn's face seemed to flatten out and grow hard. "I've told you. You start anything and I'll take you in."

Radigan measured Flynn carefully. "Don't try it, Jim. You've a wife and family. You don't want trouble because you're afraid you'll lose all that. The day you try to take me in, you've lost it."

Jim Flynn's jaw set, and slowly his feet shifted. And then he looked into Radigan's eyes and suddenly everything within him seemed to go still and cold.

Radigan was not bluffing.

"Don't push me, Tom," he said, but even as he spoke there was certainty in him that if he attempted to arrest Radigan he would be killed.

"The day you try to arrest me without cause, Jim," Radigan replied shortly, "that day you'll die. I am in the right here, and it is you who've followed off a pretty red wagon because it's new. I'm going over your head, Jim."

"What's that mean?"

"I've written to the governor, and to the sheriff. I have notified them of the situation here. My certificates of title are registered in Santa Fe, and if you interfere in this, except to run that Foley outfit off, you are an accessory after the fact of a crime."

Jim Flynn suddenly found himself with nothing to say. If Radigan had written to the sheriff and the governor, and if Radigan was in the right, then his own job was not worth a tinker's damn. At the same time he suddenly realized he had a strong distaste for a gun battle with the man who had killed Vin Cable.

At the same time the letter gave him an out and he was quick to accept it. "All right, I'll wait. I'll wait until I hear from the sheriff, and then I'll act, and if it's you I come after, I'll take you."

Tom Radigan made no reply. He knew what had

happened to Flynn and he sympathized with him. What was it Sir Francis Bacon had said, "He who hath wife and children hath given hostages to fortune, for they are impediments to great enterprise."

Well, at least they made a man think.

Radigan went inside and accepted the drink that Downey poured for him.

"Breakfast?"

"Sure."

"You killed one of them?"

"I think so."

"You did. They'll be in this morning, Tom. Some of them will be in."

"I'll think of that after breakfast."

He had written no letters, but now he did. He wrote the letters of which he had told Flynn and he wrote one other. To a Ranger captain in Tascosa, and it was an inquiry about the Foley-Thorpe outfit and their cattle.

He was on his second cup of coffee when Flynn pushed through the door. He walked immediately to Radigan's table. "You want to fight the Foley outfit?"

"Are they coming?"

"They sure are, four or five of them."

He nodded briefly. "Thanks, Jim." He had started to get up and then heard the pound of horses' hoofs and looking out the window saw the riders pulled up at the rail—five of them.

"Too late!" Flynn said angrily. "Damn it, you're too late!"

"I wanted some more coffee, anyway," he said, and sat back down.

Flynn turned sharply around. "You can get out the back door! *Quick!*"

"I like it here."

Flynn stared at him, then started to speak. His mouth opened and then snapped shut and he walked to the bar. "Give me a drink," he said hoarsely.

Radigan picked up the pot and filled his cup. Then

he leaned back in his chair and relaxed, watching the door.

Boots sounded on the boardwalk and somebody laughed.

Then the door swung wide.

four

The three cowhands who entered first were strangers to him, but the last two were Barbeau and Bitner.

They bellied up to the bar laughing and talking loudly, and obviously unaware of his presence. Whatever else the death of one of their number had done, it had not depressed them to any appreciable extent. Radigan made no move, remaining at the table, and watching them.

His trip into San Ysidro had been necessary. He wanted a final understanding with Flynn, and that unavailing, to write letters to the governor and to the county sheriff. Whatever was to come his own position must be legally secure. He anticipated no help as a result of the letters, but they did officially notify the authorities of what was transpiring and that no help was forthcoming from Flynn. After that it would be up to him, but they would have been notified of the situation and that he must take steps to preserve his property.

Flynn remained at the bar, but the cowhands appeared not to notice him. Barbeau was regaining some of his old truculence, and Bitner was, as always, a silent, morose man; but, Radigan guessed, far more dangerous than Barbeau.

Where Radigan sat the room was in partial shadow, and from the bar his face would not be readily visible. Even as he considered that, one of the cowhands glanced his way, looked off, then taken by something threatening in the silent figure at the table, he looked back. After a moment he whispered to the man next to him, and they all looked around. The cheerful conversation at the bar was suddenly stilled. Flynn straightened up and turned slightly toward them, and Bitner's attention was suddenly on Flynn.

"Where d' you stand?" Bitner's tone was casual.

"I'm the law. There'll be no trouble here."

Barbeau laughed.

Tom Radigan had not moved. Now he slowly took up the makings that lay on the table near his coffee cup and began to roll a smoke. He was waiting to see what Flynn was going to do, but if trouble came, he knew he was going to kill Bitner first . . . Bitner was the most dangerous of the lot, but the three strange punchers all looked to be tough, confident men.

Flynn persisted. "You boys have your drinks, then move along. You start any trouble in town and I'll come for you."

"He killed a man of ours."

"Maybe, but you heard what I said."

"And it don't make a bit of difference," Barbeau declared. "You can walk out of here, Sheriff, or you can keep out of it. Don't make us no difference."

"I'm staying. You start trouble and you'll go to jail."

"You'll take us?" Barbeau scoffed.

"I'll take you," Flynn replied. "Now you, Barbeau, you want to make a fight of it?"

Barbeau hesitated. He was a fair hand with a gun, but Flynn had not become a deputy sheriff for nothing, and he was not at all sure he wanted to gamble. Moreover, they had orders to stay out of trouble in town.

Flynn walked in on Barbeau. "I've told you, Barbeau. Have a drink if you want it and get out of town, but you'll start nothing here."

Barbeau hesitated and Bitner spoke up. "Let it go, Barb. Our time will come."

Shrugging, Barbeau turned toward the bar and Downey filled his glass. Radigan had been watching Downey with interest. His right hand had remained below the edge of the bar, and it was Radigan's hunch the shotgun was there. Radigan picked up the pot and filled his cup.

He was in a dangerous position. Outside of town he

would be fair game. Flynn, despite the fact that he was deputy sheriff of the county, had practically said as much. He would keep the peace here, but outside of town a man would have to fight his own battles.

Yet the black horse bore no brand they knew, and they might suspect his horse was stabled elsewhere. Radigan had a hunch they would go outside, check both ways out of town, and wait for him, and common sense told him he had no reason to buck the kind of a deck they would stack against him. He pondered the question while he waited.

Downey came around the bar. "More coffee, Tom?"

"Please."

They would be expecting him north of town, on the route back toward the ranch, yet they would have a man or men at the trail that ran southwest out of town, too. There was a point of rocks that came down to the trail a bit over a mile out of town, but just this side of that point a dim trail, scarcely visible any more, left the main road and went up through the rocks and cut back, climbing higher and higher toward Pajarito Peak, but well this side of the peak there was a break in the long ridge that divided that trail from the valley where San Ysidro lay.

If he could get out of town—if he could get to that trail—and if they let him leave town, he'd have a chance, because the logical waiting point was at the point of rocks.

He finished his cigarette and drank the remaining coffee, and then the men walked out of the saloon, and he was alone. "Thanks, Jim," he said.

"Don't thank me. I just don't want any trouble."

"All right."

Radigan got up and walked to the bar and paid Downey, who dropped the money into the cash drawer without glancing at it. "Watch yourself, Tom. They'll be waiting."

Radigan glanced out the window. Their horses were gone, but there was a man loitering across the street and up a short distance.

Radigan grinned. "God have pity on the poor sailors on such a night as this!"

Downey said, "You'll do, Tom—only those boys want you."

"Pack me a bait of grub, will you? I may be in the hills a couple of days."

"That girl didn't get hurt, did she?" Downey asked.

"No. Lot of iron in that girl, Pat. She'll be around when the chips are cashed in."

He shrugged into his coat while Downey put the last of the bundle together. Radigan was thinking of all the buildings down the street. There were four on the right side of the road, three on the left, and scattered houses back of that, lanes, barnyards, stables. The Hansen house was on the left but back from the road, and the idea came to him suddenly.

"See you," he walked out the door and closed it carefully behind him. He crossed the walk as if going away from the saloon, then turned and stepped quickly into the saddle on the black horse, swung abruptly around the saloon and behind it.

The action was swift and unexpected. The watcher across the street was caught flat-footed, but instantly he dashed across the street. Before he could round the saloon, Radigan rode from behind it and was across the street and behind a building there. He rode down into the wash, came up through the trees, walking the black in soft sand to make no noise. And then he rode directly for the Hansen place.

It was a big, old adobe with an upstairs gallery and it stood among some cottonwoods with corrals and a barn behind it. The sun was high, and Radigan walked the black along the trail, knowing the horse was unfamiliar and gambling nobody was apt to be there who would know him. He walked the horse past the house and tied in among some brush under the cottonwoods beyond the house.

From inside the house he heard a pleasant soprano voice singing an old love song. He listened for a moment, then rapped on the door. A breeze stirred the cottonwoods and they chafed their leaves with soft whispering. The singing stopped and he heard footsteps within. He shifted his weight and the floor boards creaked slightly, and the door swung open.

Angelina Foley was quite obviously astonished. He removed his hat. "How do you do, Miss Gelina? Are you receiving callers?"

Momentarily she hesitated, then she stepped back. "Come in. You startled me."

"Some of your men seemed to be in a fighting mood," he commented casually, "and I thought I'd let them cool off a bit." He smiled. "And I thought it might be a good time to get better acquainted."

"You're assuming that I wish to know you better?"

"Don't you?"

"I'm not sure." She motioned to a divan. "You have your nerve, coming here."

"Can you think of a better place?" He relaxed on the divan. From where he sat he could see the trail leading up to the ranch. "If one has to wait, why not where a man can talk to a beautiful girl?"

She waited, and he looked around the house. It was a roomy old place, cool, comfortable and quiet, yet much had been done to change it. There were curtains in the windows tonight, and a piano—how long since he had seen a piano outside of a barroom?

"You sing very well. Do you play?"

"Of course."

"Will you?"

"Mr. Radigan, if you have any business with me, please state it. I have no intention of playing for you, and I think it impudent of you to suggest it."

"It is all too rare when we hear music out here," he replied, his manner reflecting no reaction to her evident impatience. "Especially old Italian folk songs."

"You know that song?" Her surprise was evident.

"We come from many places," he replied. "You'll find among Western men some who know many things beside cows and range conditions." He paused. "Miss Gelina, I'm curious. Why did you come here?"

"Because of the land I own," she replied coldly. "What other reason could there be?"

He shrugged, turning his hat in his hand. "I was wondering. Usually folks who have a good working ranch and a herd the size of yours don't leave the place where they are. I'm wondering why you left, and why you work a bunch of hands who handle guns better than they do cows."

Angelina Foley glanced toward the door. She was alone here, with only the Mexican woman cook for company, but she was thinking rapidly, trying to discover some method of attracting some of her hands back to this ranch. Radigan had guessed shrewdly that this would be the last place they would think of looking, and moreover, every remark he made gave greater reason for worry. This was no ordinary cowhand or cattleman.

"I wrote to the governor," he said.

She stiffened. "You *what?*"

"I wrote to the governor," he repeated. "They know me in Santa Fe, and I wanted them to know what was happening here."

She was frightened, but she knew at once that they were in real trouble. This was the last thing they had expected. When they prepared to drive west out of Texas, Harvey had assured her there would be no trouble as they not only had claim to the land to which they were going but the man squatted on it would be eliminated before they arrived. She had suspected for some time that Harvey had some further idea in the back of his head, some idea for going to the New Mexico ranch. She had not inquired too much about that.

The move was essential. Her father had managed the ranch poorly, had spent too much money, and had become involved in hopeless quarrels. It was due to her own quick action and positive thinking as much as to Harvey that they had abandoned the hopeless fight and moved to New Mexico. The trail they had left behind them was not a pretty one, but due to Ross Wall they had brought the herd safely across the long, dry drive and had left behind all pursuers—left them dead.

Now, if an inquiry began there would be immediate repercussions from Texas.

Instantly she knew he must not guess her panic, and she saw that somehow she must win him over or he must be killed. Or better yet, made to disappear. If he merely disappeared there would be a period of waiting to see if he reappeared, and by that time they would be settled on the ranch with friends of their own.

"It's too bad there is trouble between us." She got up and walked to the window, and as she spoke her thoughts raced swiftly ahead, searching out a way through all the nooks and crannies of possible solutions. "You're a strong man, Tom."

"Just a cattleman."

"No, far more than that. I wish we could have met under other circumstances. A girl in my position, who has to run a ranch like a man, doesn't meet many men who are of interest to her."

She was not, she reflected, just talking. Every word was the truth. She turned suddenly and looked at him, seeing for the first time through the implication of her own words, and realizing it was true: this was the man she should have met before this.

He was a handsome man. And without doubt a courageous one. There was nothing of Harvey in him, Harvey who had an ulterior motive for everything, and who was always searching for some way to make money without work.

She crossed the room to him. Over her shoulder he saw that the road was still empty. "Tom, what do you want out of life? I mean, what are you working for?"

"I want to make that ranch pay. You have no idea what a job that is. I mean, you've come here from a Plains state where the problems are tough enough, but you know the answers to them, as I did. Up here one has to learn new answers, new ways. I'm cautious, so I came with few cattle, and I worked particularly hard to keep them alive. By the time I found the answers I'd managed to wet-nurse a small herd through two winters, and by then I could branch out a little."

"Is it that hard?"

"Worse! You're welcome to come and see for yourself if you like." He gestured with a quick dismissing wave of his hand. "Your folks probably think they've won, but we left the ranch because we didn't want to be pinned down, and we aren't worried because we know what will happen this winter. You'll lose that herd, lose everything you've got. Your hands will quit because you have easy money hands, except for Wall, and maybe a few others. Of course," he added, "you might be lucky. We might have a good winter.

His words had the ring of truth and she was worried. The herd was all she had, and if they lost it they would have nothing.

Sensing her doubt, he said, "Have you looked at that valley lately? You've had the cattle on it for several days, and the grass is about gone. You've too many cows for the range you can get."

He was the one they must be rid of, for once he was gone there would be no trouble from John Child or that girl. The girl they could destroy by implication, and Child would probably go down with her, or he could be tracked down and killed.

How to get Radigan? His appeal to the authorities frightened her, for it was the one thing they had never expected and the one thing that could destroy them. Yet if he disappeared, seemed to ride away on his own, then it would be a simple thing. The whole affair would die down and their seizure of the ranch would be an accomplished fact which a visit to Santa Fe by Harvey and herself would cement into finality. Harvey could be polished and ingratiating, and she knew what a beautiful woman could do to most men. With Radigan out of the way.

"Do we have to fight?" she protested. "I mean, do we have to be enemies?"

She came close to him. "Tom, I am sorry, I really am. Can't we end all this? You must understand how

I feel? After all, my father left the land to me, and it is all I have of his."

"I'm sorry."

She looked up at him, making her eyes wide, her lips parted a little. "Tom, please! We mustn't be enemies!"

He looked down at him and suddenly she felt he was laughing at her. He made no move to take her into his arms, although the invitation was there, nor did he move away. He just looked down into her eyes and said quietly. "We need not be enemies. I wish it wasn't that way, so why don't you give up this notion and move away?"

She was furious. Her anger flashed wickedly for an instant, and then she drew back, and smiled quickly, almost sharply at him. "No! I couldn't do that. It—it would be almost a betrayal. Of my father, I mean."

She turned away from him and walked to the window. Glancing past her he saw the road was still empty. Suddenly he was aware that she, too, was watching that road, which meant she was either expecting or hoping for someone.

She knew she must stall, she must find some way to keep him from leaving until someone came. She knew now there was no other way: he must be killed. Either killed here or trailed until he could be killed elsewhere.

There was no doubt in her now, no hesitation. She was startled at that. It had been one thing to agree to the killing of an unknown squatter, quite another to order the slaying of a man she knew and with whom she had talked. Yet there was no desire to wait, to think it out. If she was to own that ranch, Tom Radigan must be killed. It was simple as that.

Her father had been the weak one. He got them into fights but always hesitated, moved too slow, or talked too much. Those were mistakes she did not intend to make. This was her land, and without it she was no one, and she had nothing. With it she could hide the stolen cattle far back in those hard-to-find valleys where Ross Wall said Radigan's cattle were, and if they were trailed here, they could assume utter innocence and there would be no evidence.

Radigan picked up his hat. "I'll be going now." He was growing increasingly nervous. There was no telling what a woman would do, and her men might be coming at any time, and by now they would have given up the search close to town. He might make it to the trail he wanted without being seen.

Desperately she tried to think of something to keep him, but he moved to the door and stepped out onto the porch. As he did so she saw Barbeau, gun in hand, standing by the porch, and she reached out quickly and grabbed Radigan's gun arm with both hands, just as Barbeau's pistol came to bear on him. She grasped his arm with desperate energy and fearful that he would draw a gun, she jerked him off balance just as Barbeau fired.

The bullet smashed into the doorjamb, missing Radigan by inches, and he reached across with his left hand and drew the Colt, flipping it around and firing just as Barbeau got off his second shot.

Barbeau, worried for fear of hitting Angelina, and frightened because of his miss, missed again by an even wider margin. And then Radigan's bullet slammed into him, knocking him sidewise. Jerking free, Radigan sent Angelina staggering and sprang off the porch.

Barbeau, shot through the shoulder, had dropped his gun. He was reaching for it with his left hand when Radigan fired again. He had fired into Barbeau's body, but the bullet hit the heavy buckle at an angle and glanced off, knocking the wind out of Barbeau and tearing a wicked gash in his forearm, and then Radigan was around the house and running for his horse.

A rifle fired from the house and he dove for the brush, falling on his hands as a second bullet clipped brush ahead of him. He rolled over, catching a quick glimpse of Angelina herself standing near the porch working the lever on the Winchester. His roll had put him on hands and feet and he dove forward in a plunging run that crashed him into the brush. Dodging quickly to change his line of travel he reached the black. The horse was frightened and it was a wild minute before he could get a foot into stirrup and swing to the saddle. Behind him another rifle shot cut the brush and he heard running feet. Then the black was running, heading toward the San Ysidro Trail, yet an instant later, when the horse swung up on a slight rise he saw a dozen horsemen fanned out between him and the trail, coming fast.

There was no hope for it. He swung the black on his hind feet and headed east at a dead run.

There was another rifle shot as he swung past the ranch. And dead ahead of him, barring his escape to the northeast, was the gigantic wall of rock that towered up in cliffs fifteen hundred feet high: the cliffs themselves, he knew, were not that high, but it was a climb up to them and hopeless when he got there. There were many convolutions in those cliffs, but he knew there was no way up or through them.

The black was a fast horse and was running all out, but the black was not grain-fed like his own horses and how much it could take he could not begin to guess. Behind him the fanned-out riders were bunching except for a couple who had continued to ride due east, evidently to prevent any attempt at escape to the south, and to eventually cut him off in the east.

Ahead of him a great promontory of the escarpment reached out into the flatlands as if to cut off his escape. If those riders who continued to ride east encountered no ravines they would be riding a trail that would meet that promontory and so cut him off, completely. Past it he seemed to remember the mouth of Hondo Canyon opened wide, offering access to the hills to the north. If he reached that point of rocks first, he might escape, and if he did not, then it was a back-to-the-wall fight until his ammunition gave out and they closed in on him. All he could then hope for was to take some of them with him.

Using his spurs, he raced the black for the point. The wind whipped his face, and his hat blew off and hung to the back of his neck by the chin strap. The black was lathering, but running freely and with no break in its stride. Behind him there were occasional shots, but it would be merest chance if one hit him at this pace.

He did not look back, but his glance went again and again to the riders who were running only a little behind him and on his right. On his left the wall of the mountain closed in nearer and nearer. The black horse ran like a frightened rabbit, ducking and dodging or jumping mesquite clumps, running as if it knew that death ran close behind.

A bullet whipped by so close it frightened him and he jerked his head as if from an angry bee. The point of rock loomed up ahead of him, the black's feet spurned the sand beneath and the cold wind cut through his shirt. Now the riders on his right were angling toward him: within the next few minutes he would know.

And then he did know. They were going to meet him right there. They had to.

It was then he drew his gun. He palmed the Colt and tried a fast shot at the nearest man's horse. He fired three times as rapidly as he could trigger the Colt, and suddenly the horse shied, slowed an instant. It was not a hit, just a disconcertingly close bullet, but the startled horse slowed and the rider following plunged into him, and in that instant of confusion and plunging horses, Radigan went around the point on a dead run.

Hondo Canyon opened wide before him, a mile wide at the mouth but rapidly narrowing into a mere cleft in the rocks. The only trails he knew ended in dead ends at the head of the canyons, but there might be a chance on the left, or western canyon. He ran the black up the canyon, then sighting split in the wall on his right he put the horse up the steep slope. It plunged desperately and then, nearly to the top, staggered and almost fell. Radigan swung from the saddle and holding the reins scrambled toward the top. Behind him a shot exploded and a bullet clipped a fragment of rock within inches of him. Stung by fragments, the black lunged ahead and they were over the rim.

Sliding his Winchester from the scabbard, Radigan dropped near a fallen log and snapped a quick shot into the plunging horses below. A man screamed and he levered shots into the group as swiftly as he could get off the shots.

A horse went down, kicking and fighting, and the riders scattered for shelter. A bullet from his Winchester kicked sand at the heels of one, knocked another loose from his saddle. The man fell, his boot caught in the stirrup and the horse ran with him, dragging the fallen man by his caught foot.

Crawling back, Radigan got slowly to his feet. Despite the chill he was bathed in sweat and the black was streaked with lather and trembling. Catching up the reins, Radigan walked slowly away under the trees. It was just past noon.

He walked steadily, leading the horse, knowing they would first catch the horse that was dragging the rider, and then they would try to find another way up. They would suspect him of having left, but they would not be sure, and they would be delayed. They might, although he scarcely hoped it would be so, break off the chase for the time. He had hit a man and a horse, perhaps two men. And the dragged man, if still alive, would be in no condition to fight.

It was a good day's work. Three to four of them out of action at least, and a lot of luck.

On his right there was a great ridge of rock shaped like a great ship. Keeping to shelving sheets of rock he left no trail to speak of, and moved steadily along. After awhile he mounted up.

This was wild, relatively unknown country to him, although John Child had told him there was a spring up in these mountains called Ojo del Oso. With luck he would find it.

Scarcely a half-hour later he did find it. He refilled his canteen there, and watered the black, rubbing him down with a handful of mesquite. He could not see his back trail, and in these rocks there would be no dust plume to indicate pursuit, nonetheless he must act as if

there was pursuit. To the north the mountains towered
high, and west of him there were steep cliffs and canyons to cut him off. His only route lay to the east or
northeast, but by riding northeast he might swing
around to the hideout where John Child and Gretchen
waited.

Far off, perhaps twenty to twenty-five miles east, was
the canyon of the Rio Grande, and the finger canyons
of Frijole and Pajarito Creeks pointed the way to the
mother river.

North he rode, ever higher and ever rougher the
country, and colder the wind. It was a wild and lonely
land. Several times he startled deer, and once saw a
grizzly. It stood on its hind legs for a better view of
him, and watched him from a hundred yards away as
he rode by.

He reloaded his six-gun—the first time since he could
remember that he had waited so long to load up after
firing. It had become an almost automatic reaction, yet
back there he had had no time. The afternoon lost itself against the mountains and inquiring shadows crept
down from the hidden canyons, and peered at him from
under the towering trees. A searching wind found him
with its cold fingers, and he patted the black and
talked softly to it, and the black twitched a responsive
ear to his words.

It was cold, so very cold, and the only way lay up
into the still colder regions among the high peaks and
across the lonely, wind-swept plateaus where no man
rode willingly. He sagged in the saddle, and the black
plodded on, all the splendid fire gone from its muscles.

Under a ghostly, lightning-struck pine, he swung
down. But he did not stop, walking on, responding to
the resentful tug on the bridle by a harder tug. He
followed the contour of the hills, working steadily north.
A few flakes of snow fell.

Before him the view opened out showing a mighty
panorama of rugged mountains and canyons lost in
darkness, of forests blasted by lightning and the gray,
bleached bones of long dead trees. Under the low gray

clouds the scene was weirdly somber and majestic. The higher ridges and peaks vanished in the low clouds and before him the wide shelf upon which he rode stretched out, bare and unpromising.

From behind his saddle he took his sheepskin coat and shrugged into it. Fortunately it was split high in the back so he could wear it while riding: only he did not ride now, but strode out at a fast pace, heading along the vast shoulder of the mountain. On his right a canyon dropped away, probably hundreds of feet to a stream at the bottom, but he walked on, looking ahead for some place that promised a camp for the night.

Darkness crept out from the icy peaks and night fell. Still he stumbled on, the horse plodding along behind him, and when he came at last to a place for camping, it was only a corner among the rocks and trees but it offered shelter from the wind.

In a V where two huge boulders came together he built his fire, and facing it he built a lean-to of evergreen boughs where the faces of the rocks would reflect the heat of the fire into the shelter. By weaving boughs among the living boughs of the trees he made a crude shelter for the black horse, and some of the heat would reach it there. Of dead wood there was more than sufficient, and he made a good fire to warm the rocks, then carried his saddle and gear into the lean-to.

With a handful of evergreen needles he rubbed down the black horse and gathered snow to melt for coffee, preferring to keep what water he had in the canteen. It was very cold. He unwrapped the food packed for him by Downey at the saloon, and then hung a feedbag on the black with a little corn he had carried behind the saddle.

He had a ground sheet and two blankets which he unrolled on a bed made of boughs. He sat within the lean-to and ate, drinking his coffee and wondering about John Child and Gretchen. Had they been discovered? It was unlikely.

Snow began to fall. Not the intermittent flakes but fine, icy particles, and it did not stop but continued. A wolf howled somewhere out in the forest and the black horse shifted his feet uneasily. Radigan spoke to the horse and stretched his hands toward the eager flames. From time to time he added a stick, and it was very cold, the wind coming around the boulders and plucking at the fire, stirring it with irritable fingers.

The icy snow rattled on the rocks and the dried branches or fell whispering into the evergreens. He was high on the mountainside, perhaps 8,500 feet. Finally he drank another cup of coffee laced with whisky and then crawled into the bed.

Twice during the night he crawled out, shivering with cold, to replenish the fire, and the last time it was so cold and so near to dawn that he stayed up, huddling over the fire. He brought the black in closer and built up the fire. Outside a heavy blanket of snow lay over everything, and it would have covered any trail he might have left. Up to this point, anyway. If they came this far they were going to have a cinch following him.

Day came reluctantly, and Radigan tugged on his boots again and stirred about, making coffee and warming water for the horse. He ate some cold beef and drank scalding coffee, and finally, after warming the blanket over the fire, he saddled up and packed his bed.

In the cold, white light of early dawn he moved out into a world where everything had changed during the night. The black was a good mountain horse and he walked delicately, not trusting the snow. He rode what he estimated to be six miles, riding north but pushed farther east by the terrain, and suddenly he came out of the trees and drew up looking over a magnificent bowl among the hills.

It was obviously what remained of a magnificent and gigantic volcanic crater. The floor of the valley was at least five hundred feet below the point where he sat his horse, and was surrounded by clumps of spruce and aspen that gave way to a thick growth of these trees mingled with stands of pine. In the summer this would be an enormous meadow, and looking away into the distance he could see it was at least twenty miles in length, or close to it. Within the crater there must be more than one hundred and fifty square miles of territory.

The black horse seemed as surprised as he himself, pricking its ears at the vast valley that lay before them. This was without doubt the same valley of which the Indians had told stories long ago.

Skirting the valley he found a way down to the bottom, and when he reached it he moved out across the snow. Near the cliffs the snow had drifted in spots, but for the most part the vast plain was but thinly covered. He scuffed the snow away and found the grass below was thick, cured on the stem, and good hay. While he looked around the black began to crop the brown grass.

Suddenly he realized this was the place he had been seeking. Here he could graze a lot of cattle, and this rich grass would provide better feed than any of the lower prairies. Undoubtedly his own ranch lay only a few miles to the westward, and within an easy drive of this place. There was a small stream that ran through the bottom of the valley, so water was no problem. He knew suddenly that this was where he would drift his own cattle if the fight became worse.

At the valley where their remuda was corralled he roped a fresh horse. John Child had been there since the snow, and Radigan trailed him back to their hideout through the darkening hours of the third day. He was within a short distance of the place when he heard a shell jacked into a chamber and he froze in place. "It's all right!" he called. "It's me!"

"I see you." It was Coker. He stepped down into the trail, a wide grin on his face. "Come on up. You got comp'ny."

For an instant he felt like reining around and running for it, but there wasn't a chance. He was fairly caught between the walls of the canyon, plain to see against the new-fallen snow, and he knew that Coker would like nothing better than an excuse to kill him.

His hands were numb with cold or he might have

tried for a gun. He put his right hand under his armpit to warm the fingers. There was yet time. And there was a chance. As long as he had a gun, there was a chance.

They were at the cave. He recognized the bulky body of Ross Wall, and a squat puncher named Jones who had been in the saloon at San Ysidro when Flynn had backed them down. He was fairly caught.

John Child was there, seated against a wall, his hands tied behind him. And Gretchen was there, but her hands were untied and she was cooking.

"I was hopin' you wouldn't come back," Child commented.

"Cold out there." He swung down stiffly. "We've had a snow."

"Radigan," Ross Wall was brusque. "You've got feed stacked somewhere. We want to know where."

"Sorry."

Coker grinned at him. "Ross, let me have him. I can get it from him."

Radigan merely glanced at him. "You couldn't get anything from me," he said. "I wouldn't give you the time of day."

Wall interrupted Coker's reply with an impatient gesture. "You've had it, Radigan. I can't do a thing for you. Maybe if you talk I can get these others off, but I'll tell you right now that we have orders to lose your body in one of those canyons north of here where nobody will find it."

"We had a visitor," Child commented.

"Shut up!" Coker turned sharply around.

Gretchen sensed it was something Radigan should know. She looked up from the fire. "He said he'd be back," she said.

Coker turned on her angrily. "You, too! Shut your mouth!"

Ross Wall glanced at Coker. "That'll do," he said. "You'll not talk to a lady that way."

"She's no lady," Coker retorted. "She's—!"

Gretchen grabbed a stick from the fire and swung the burning end at Coker's face. He sprang back, but not fast enough and the stick caught him across the mouth. He staggered off balance and fell, crying out with pain and grasping his burned lips.

Gretchen stood up. "I'll cook for you," she said to Wall, "because you're hungry men, but I won't take any slander from such as he is."

Coker was moaning and holding his mouth. Wall merely glanced at him. "Go back to your cooking," he said.

She went back to the fire, and moved a pot more firmly into position on some stones in the fire. Then she said, "The man was Loren Pike. He said he and Charlie Cade were at Loma Coyote."

Wall's eyes showed his sudden attention. "Did you say Loren Pike? The Ranger?"

"He was a Ranger," Radigan explained. "About the time I was. He left the outfit to settle a personal quarrel."

"What are they doing here?"

"Friends of mine. I told you I was a Ranger, too. Fact is, I wrote to the Rangers in Tascosa just the other day."

Radigan could see the idea did not please Ross Wall. The foreman walked to the mouth of the cave where Radigan's horse still stood. For several minutes he stood there, staring down the darkening canyon, and Radigan watched him while Coker moaned and swore in a corner of the cave, holding his mouth with both hands.

Wall knew very well that many of the Rangers stuck together through thick and thin, and often after they had left the service they returned to help one another, and the thought gave him no pleasure. More than that, Loren Pike was a known man, a good man with a gun who had been active in running down cattle thieves. Moreover, he had been cousin to the Bannings with whom the Foley outfit had been feuding. Had he followed them?

"Who's Cade?" he asked.

"Friend of mine. We rode together, a year or two. If

he don't find me here he's going to be mighty unhappy."

"What are two men?" It was the stocky puncher who spoke.

"Either one of them would take your pelt and tack it on the barn door without raising a sweat," Radigan told him.

The more Ross Wall considered the situation the less he liked it. Handling Angelina Foley was bad enough, but after that slick-talking Harvey Thorpe came home there was no holding her, and the outfit had gone from one trouble to another. He knew little about her claim to the present land except that her father had always talked of a ranch he owned in New Mexico.

The snow would make feed a real problem, and unless they found the feed that Radigan had stacked against the bad months they were going to lose a lot of cattle. Matter of fact, they were going to lose some anyway. Now this.

If those men were coming back they would have to be killed too, for they would ask questions that must not be asked. And they would know too much. Maybe they already knew.

"They know about this fight?" he asked Child.

"What d' you suppose we talked about?"

He might have guessed it. Still, it might be some time before they came back, and he had heard of Loma Coyote. Suppose he detached four or five men to ride up there and ambush the two? But where would it end? When a man tried to solve his problems with a killing it always led to still another. He swore softly, looking out at the gathering night, knowing there would have to be a showdown with Thorpe, and not relishing the thought.

Wall had his orders. Find Tom Radigan and get rid of him. Get rid of him so he could never be found again. And that was all very well, but with such men as Pike and Cade involved, the disappearance of Radigan might easily begin another blood feud. How could a man make a ranch pay under such circumstances? He stared downcanyon gloomily. For that matter, how could anyone make a ranch pay in this country? Radigan said he knew how, but Ross Wall had heard men talk big before.

Gretchen took the first plate of food to Radigan, and the second to John Child, placing it on the ground and then coolly untying his hands.

Child chafed his hands and wrists, glancing over at Radigan who sat quietly. The squat puncher was watching them with a rifle across his knees. Ross Wall turned and walked back into the cave, accepting his food with a quiet thanks, and staring at it somberly before he started to eat.

Radigan had been disarmed, but his weapons lay across from him within easy reach, almost as if he were being tempted to try for them. From Coker's earlier attitude and the manner of the others now, Radigan was sure he was marked for death and, in fact, could see no other alternative for the Foley outfit. He moved with great care, always keeping his hands in view, and while he ate he was thinking, working around the herd of his thoughts trying to get a rope on the one he needed . . . a way out.

So far they had come off second best in the fighting, but that was pure unadulterated luck, as he would have been the first to admit. He had thrown his shots at the horses with only hope that they would land and that they had done what he hoped had been the purest chance.

Flynn had kept him out of a bad spot in San Ysidro, and his flight into the mountains and the subsequent snow had helped to get him away from the fight scot-free. He was under no illusions as to the outcome of such a fight if everything else went as it usually did.

A cold wind was blowing from the north. "This wind holds, you'll have a drift, your cattle will drift clean out of the country."

Wall shot him a sullen glance and made no reply. Trust a cattleman to be thinking of that.

Radigan finished his meal, accepted more coffee, and

began to roll a smoke. He wanted to keep his hands free, and wanted Child's free, so he tried to keep Wall thinking, worrying. "Look, Ross," he said conversationally, "why not let the herd drift? Why don't you boys follow it out of the country? This is a fight you can't win, and if you kill us, how will you find the feed? Believe me, you can look for a long time, and unless you're mighty lucky, you'd not find it, and you know as well as I do that you're working on a mighty slim margin."

He paused and, lifting the cigarette to his lips, shot a glance at the nearest gun, and knew it was too far. But the cowhand named Coker was close. He was not eating, but had rubbed some grease on his burned and swollen lips. If he could drop on his side and grab Coker, reaching around him for his gun, he might manage it. But the chance was too great.

"Take it from me, Loren Pike and Charlie Cade will be back, and Cade owes a lot to me. So does Pike. They won't come riding into a trap, either. They'll come riding down here expecting a full-scale war, and they'll be loaded for bear.

"Why, Ross, up there at Loma Coyote there's eight or ten of the toughest fighting men in the country, and all they need to know is there's some cattle down here they can have for the taking, and they'll trail along with Loren Pike.

"You ever hear of Adam Stark? He's the best rifle shot in this part of the country. Out of Tennessee by way of Texas, and a good man anywhere. Well, Adam is up there at Loma Coyote, and he's been itching to get into this fight. Ask John Child there—he's a close friend of John's—and he's been wanting to come down. Figure it out for yourself. These boys know the terrain, they know cattle, and you can just bet that whatever cattle get through the winter will be driven off.

"You know something, Ross? All those brands don't look so good, and I've been wondering how they'd look if a man skinned one of those steers and checked that brand from the back of the hide. I'm wondering what brand would show up."

"Shut up!" Ross Wall turned angrily. "You talk too damn' much!"

"I'll shut him up," Coker said. "You just give me the word, and I'll shut him up!" He mumbled the words through puffed lips. "I'll kill him!"

The fire crackled, and outside the snow fell steadily. No use trying a break now, for a man could be tracked easily unless he had a good enough start for the snow to fill his tracks. There was nothing to do but to wait, and Radigan settled back. He was good at waiting, better than any Indian, as John Child had often said. Well, this was a time to see just how good he was. Moreover, he was beginning to get an idea of how he could handle the situation, just a glimmer of an idea.

Firelight flickered on their faces, gleamed on gun barrels and buckles, and outside the snow fell softly into the cushiony silence. The opening of the overhang was a black wall streaked with the slow fall of snow. Ross Wall stared gloomily into the fire and Radigan had noted the habit before and filed it for future reference. A man who stares into a fire is blind when he looks into the darkness, for a moment at least. And who needed more?

If they hadn't found his feed by now there was small chance they would find it with this snow in the passes. He knew where the snow drifted, and the few routes there were that might be used. During the four years of residence on the ranch he had learned to plan his campaigns against the elements as a good general plans his strategy during a war. It was the price of survival.

Yet sometimes these first falls of snow did not last, but were swept away by the first change in the weather, and such might be the case with this one, and even a brief thaw might open up the passes, even if not for long.

The squat cowpuncher had leaned back against the wall, partly pillowed on his own saddle, and was snoring gently. Coker stared sullenly at Gretchen, and said nothing at all, and there was no light anywhere but the light from the flickering fire. Radigan poked a stick into the coals and watched it ignite, and he had a hunch that Wall had been told to find him and finish him off, and that Wall had no stomach for it. The big foreman was a cattleman, and in fighting he might kill a man, but he was no murderer.

Under the circumstances to attempt an escape could result only in death, and in the close quarters of the cave, a wild bullet might kill anyone. So could a ricochet. Gretchen would be in as great danger as any of them, perhaps more so, considering the cold hatred obvious in Coker.

The snow fell steadily, and Radigan knew if it continued through the night it would be extremely difficult if not impossible to get out of the canyon. And three additional mouths would make great inroads on their food supply.

A flurry of wind blew into the cave mouth and danced the flames. A spark flew near the sack of corn for the horses, and Child reached over and put it out. It was very late.

Ross Wall got up and walked to the cave mouth and looked out, and when he came back his face was lined with worry. "How deep can it get in these canyons?"

"Here?" Radigan shrugged. "In a snow like this, counting for snow drifted by the wind, it might get eight to ten feet deep, and probably much less. But it often gets twenty feet deep in these canyons in the winter. Always danger of slides off the peaks, too."

His body was tired and he leaned back against the wall, yet the fatigue had not spread to his mind and he knew, whatever happened, he must remain alert. Yet if John Child was awake . . . He glanced over at the Indian and indicated by sign language that he must rest. Child nodded and Radigan settled himself more carefully, and as he did so he marked in his mind the position of the guns.

Despite the fire it was cold in the cave for there was no great depth to the overhang, and although the space was partly shielded by trees and undergrowth these were scant protection from the wind. Huddled under his blanket, Radigan slept fitfully, awakening at times to listen to the rising wind, the crackle of the fire, or the breaking of sticks as John Child replenished the flames. Without the necessity for conversation they had accepted the task of keeping the fire going, and nobody had offered any argument against their doing it, yet each understood the reason was not one of being helpful, but merely to offer them a little freedom of movement that might, in time, be utilized.

Ross Wall did not sleep. He sat staring at the flames or got to his feet and paced back and forth. Radigan could appreciate his concern, for downcountry there were nearly three thousand cattle, poorly fed these last few days, and only too ready to drift. Moreover, nobody was with those cattle who felt sufficient responsibility. They might, if sheltered from the wind, remain close against the canyon walls throughout the storm, and they might again begin to drift.

Radigan glanced nearby at the huddled, sleeping form of Gretchen. Only she was not sleeping. She was looking at him from wide blue eyes and, as she looked, she moved something under the covers and he saw the butt of a pistol, momentarily revealed, then hidden away beneath the blanket.

A pistol.

He considered it with care. How Gretchen had managed to secure it, he could not guess, but it was further evidence that she was thinking all the time. He had to have that gun, but he had to have it only at the right time and the right place. For the time being it was safer with Gretchen, who was less likely to be searched.

Attempting to return to sleep he found it impossible, for now that he was fully awake the cold of the rock floor of the cave was such as to permit no sleep. He threw off the blanket and shrugged into his sheepskin coat. "Get some sleep, John," he advised. "I'll tend the fire."

Coker watched him from under heavy lids. The gunman's lips were in frightful condition, swollen and inflamed with great blisters where the burn had left its mark. He dared not change expression, and occasionally when some involuntary movement caused his face to twitch he gasped with pain.

The fuel supply was growing small, so drawing on his gloves, Radigan walked to the edge of the overhang and stepped out into the snow. He heard sharp movement behind him, and the click of a back-drawn gun hammer but he coolly began breaking branches from one of the deadfalls he had brought near for fuel.

This, he reflected, was one way it might be done. If one man was asleep and he could get the other to turn his back on the cave—it was a chance. Also, he thought, he might make a break for it in the snow, even without a gun. There was a rifle and three pistols at the cache on the mesa back of the ranch, and there was another rifle and a shotgun in the cache near San Antonio Valley. There was food in both places.

That was one way it could be done, but he could not go alone. He trusted Wall to prevent any attack upon Gretchen, but suppose Ross Wall had to leave her alone with Coker and the other man? Coker was filled with a hatred only held in check by Wall's presence.

For the first time he began to think seriously of the problem of escape. Until now he had needed rest, until now he had wanted to learn more of their position, but now he knew the time was drawing near when they must escape. Wall, he was sure, had been told to kill them, and while he might delay, he might just ride off and leave them to Coker. He brought an armful of wood close to the fire, but he did not bring in too much.

It would soon be day, and the snow was still falling. There would be no chance to get the horses, no chance to get food. They must rely upon their chance of getting to the nearest cache, but in this snow a man on snowshoes could move faster than a horse.

Snowshoes.

A man could contrive snowshoes. Long ago, he had

been shown how to do it by an Indian. Not snowshoes for fast going, but shoes that would at least keep a man on the surface.

At first they would have to move fast, and that meant they must get out of the canyon they were in. Glancing downcanyon he studied the walls and the trees. The snow here must be at least four feet deep, and in places deeper. Wind flurries whipped snow into the canyon that drifted there and remained. When the time came to move, it would have to be a quick move. Quick and decisive.

Radigan walked in and seated himself close to the fire. He held his hands out to the fire, but as he moved them out he moved his left hand, palm down, in a slight downward movement, then did the same, only farther out, with his right and repeated with his left. To a casual observer he might only be stretching his arms in a way to draw his sleeves back, but Radigan knew that John Child had caught the Indian sign language for "walk."

A moment later he turned his hand up and drew the sleeve back a little, and managed to hold three fingers alone as he did so.

Child, sitting across the fire, appeared half-asleep. Radigan glanced at Gretchen who was watching him, and as she caught his eye she nodded slightly, indicating she understood. He had not expected her to know sign language but it was the sort of thing John Child would be apt to teach a youngster, and which a youngster would want to know.

Suddenly Ross Wall got up and walked to the mouth of the overhang. "This ain't going to ease up," he said, "and there's not enough grub to last out a bad storm."

He turned to Radigan. "How far is it to the ranch from here?"

"Might be eight miles, almost due south."

"It's colder, and we've not grub enough to last out the day. We could all die here."

"That's right. And you wait much longer and that

snow will be so deep you can't get out. Fact is, you may not make it now."

"Eight miles ain't far," Coker scoffed. "I could walk it on my hands."

Radigan ignored him and addressed his remarks to Wall. "In places this snow will be drifted up to the lower limbs of the trees, sometimes eight feet deep. Believe me, it doesn't take long in this country with no wind to sweep much of it clear."

Not long, he told himself, but still there are places. He was thinking of them now, and knew that if the right break came they would take one of them for the first brief distance, then right into the deep woods and make some snowshoes.

"I'll go," Wall said suddenly. "Mine's the best horse, and I've got a chance to get through."

Coker was staring at Gretchen, a hard satisfaction in his eyes. He would be left in charge. Or he could take charge. After that he would kill Child and Radigan. Radigan could almost see his mind working, and he could tell from the way Wall averted his eyes from them that he was thinking the same thing.

"Something else you boys didn't know about this country that you're going to find out mighty fast," Radigan commented. "Those light cow ponies you use in Texas are no good in heavy snow. It takes a horse with muscle and bone to handle it, the Montana kind of horses."

"We'll make out." Wall gathered his gear, then plunged out into the snow.

When he came back he was leading his horse, and he stood it inside the overhang while he brushed off the snow and put a blanket on, then he saddled up. Radigan watched him critically. Wall did not think of warming the bit, and the horse fought it until Wall finally bridled the horse with the help of Coker.

"You should have warmed that bit," Radigan told them, and Wall turned angrily.

"You talk too damn' much!" he flared. "There's other men handled stock besides you."

"Some people never learn," Radigan replied, grinning.

For a moment he thought Wall would strike him. The big foreman took an angry step forward, and Radigan merely looked up at him, smiling. Wall stared at him for a moment, then turned sharply away.

"You know, Ross," Radigan said, "if we'd worked for the same outfit we'd have gotten along all right."

Wall said nothing nor did he face around, and Radigan said quietly, "I wonder how you'll face yourself after this? I wonder how you'll sleep at night?"

For an instant Wall stopped gathering his gear, standing absolutely still. When Radigan next saw his face it was white, but he did not look at any of them. Merely stepping into the saddle, and then he said, "Coker, you and Gorman stay here. I'll send some grub back up right away, and some of the boys will break trail for you to come out. You take care of the prisoners."

"Sure," Coker was grinning. "I'll take care of them. Harvey told me just how to take care of them."

Without a word Ross Wall rode out into the snow. There was a narrow ledge along the wall that he could ride downcanyon for a short distance, and below the canyon there was some flat ground where the snow would not be so deep. Yet he had gone no more than a hundred yards before he knew he was in trouble.

The horse stepped off the ledge and went belly-deep in the snow, then deeper. Floundering desperately, the gelding fought his way down the canyon to the open ground, jumping and plunging. Ross Wall reined in and looked south, scowling at the rough, broken country, much of it heavily forested, and for the first time he was afraid.

It was cold. In the cave he had not realized how cold. It was very still, yet there was already frost on the horse, and he realized anew that Radigan had been right. His horse was light and fast, an excellent cow horse, but lacked the sheer power for bucking heavy drifts. It was bitterly cold, and the snow still fell. A man could die in this country.

He was not going back. He had no desire to face what was to happen in that cave. Thorpe wanted it to happen, and maybe even Angelina Foley wanted it, but he was no killer, no murderer. As for Coker, he would be in no hurry to send men back. Let the man live with himself a little. It would do him good, and there was food enough for another couple of days for two men, if they were careful.

Suddenly, from behind him he heard a shot. It was faint. It was far away, but it was a gunshot. Coker had wasted no time.

five

Coker simply turned and fired. But he turned too fast and shot too quick, and his bullet went where Radigan had just been.

For Radigan had been completely fooled. He expected Coker to talk because Coker was that sort of man. It was his pattern to play the big man for a few minutes before he killed, but Coker simply spun around and fired, throwing his bullet fast and considering the turn, with amazing accuracy.

Only the fire was sinking and Radigan had dropped to a squatting position to add fuel, and the bullet cut the air right over his head.

Yet as he spun and fired, Radigan threw himself forward and grabbing the gun that Gretchen thrust at him he rolled completely over and fired.

And missed.

It was point-blank range but he was moving and made the same mistake Coker had made by firing too quickly. But his second shot was faster, and it ripped upward into Coker's throat, ranging upward and outward to emerge just above the gunman's ear.

Coker had been so sure—and he was eager to make Gretchen suffer for his swollen and burned lips—he had turned and fired and then he was dying on his feet with blood gushing from his mouth and a puzzled expression as if he could not comprehend what had happened.

He had automatically fired a second time and the bullet had smashed into the fire, scattering sparks, but then the gun slid from his fingers and he tried to speak, staring at Radigan with dawning horror in his eyes, realizing in that last awful moment that he was dying.

His knees sagged then and he fell face forward with his feet in the snow at the entrance and his head toward the fire, and Radigan turned with his gun ready and saw Gorman stretched out on the floor with blood trickling from a split scalp where Child had clubbed him with a chunk of firewood.

Gretchen was a sickly pale, and she turned quickly from the dead man at the cave mouth and said, "We'll need a hot meal." She paused then and seemed to stiffen herself. "I've got to—"

Radigan caught her as she started to faint and she clung to him an instant, fighting it off. "I'm sorry," she said. "I'll be all right."

Child had picked up a Winchester. "D' you suppose Wall heard those shots?"

"He heard them. But he won't be back."

Child walked to the opening and caught Coker by the foot, dragging him out into the snow where he lay face down. Then he walked back and began methodically to sort the gear in the cave and pack for a leave-taking.

Radigan indicated Gorman. "Leave him some grub. We'll soon be at the cache, and he's done us no harm."

Radigan went to Coker's body and pulled off the cartridge belt and shucked the shells from the loops. The gun Gretchen had tossed him had been his own, and now he retrieved his belt and holstered the gun after reloading. He found his Winchester, checked the barrel and the loads, and then took his bowie knife and went to the trees to cut some branches.

He cut four of them, then went to another tree for two more. Each of these was about seven feet long and slender, whiplike. Over the fire he warmed them after stripping away the shorter branches that held the needles. When he had warmed them carefully he took one and working with it carefully he bent the whiplike end around and lashed it to its own base in a rough oval.

With strips of rawhide he made a web back and forth across the oval, and John Child began working on a second shoe. When Gretchen had their food ready, they ate in silence, then returned to their work. It was at this point that Gorman came to.

He opened his eyes and stared up at the hanging roof, then sat up abruptly, catching his head in both hands from a sudden throb of pain. Stupidly, he looked around.

His eyes found the body of Coker, then looked quickly around for Wall, who had left when he was half-asleep. Finally they came to rest on Radigan.

"You start anything and you join your friend out there. Sit tight and we'll leave you grub enough to last a couple of days. There's fuel enough for weeks, and if you leave here, you're crazy."

Gorman nodded to indicate Coker. "I had no use for the man."

"All right." Radigan was brusque. "You stay out of this and we've no quarrel with you, get into it and you can follow Coker."

Gorman made no reply, but lay down and turned his face to the wall.

It was afternoon before they got away. Radigan took the lead and headed south at a good clip. All he asked the snowshoes was that they see them through to the food cache on the mesa near the ranch.

He set an easy pace. There are things a man learns about the cold, and the first one is never to work up a sweat, for when a sweating man slows down or stops the sweat freezes inside his clothing, forming a thin coating of ice near the skin. After that, unless one finds shelter quickly, it is only a matter of time.

He had also learned not to dress too heavily, but to wear the garments loose so they form a cushion of warm air next to the body. The Eskimos knew these things long ago, and so did the nothern Indians, and a man can live long in any kind of country if he will use his common sense and learn what he can.

It was very cold but the air was clear. They were above eight thousand feet, and at this low temperature and in the clear air sounds could be heard for miles.

But Radigan knew the time had now come to push the fight if ever they were to push it. The cold was their greatest asset for they understood cold and he doubted if any of the Foley-Thorpe outfit did.

Somewhere below them and to the east Ross Wall would be working his way through the deep snow to the ranch, and by this time he would begin to realize some of the things Radigan had told him. That light horse would not be able to carry a heavy man far in this deep snow, and Wall would be lucky if he was not afoot by another hour, or even by now.

In good weather he could have covered that eight to ten miles in a couple of hours, but now he would have to seek out places where the earth had blown clear of snow, and he might be miles out of his way. If he made it by dark he would be lucky. Radigan said as much.

"If he makes it at all, he'll be lucky," Child said grimly.

They walked on. The going was slow, but after their muscles warmed up they moved more easily, and Radigan paused often to conserve their strength. He knew the country well and kept to high ridges where the travel was easier, always pointing toward the mesa back of the ranch.

The wind picked up and blew cold, whining among the tall pines like lost banshees, or moaning low among the icy brush and around the strange rock formations. The sky became a flat gray, unbroken expanse that told them nothing, and they came down off the ridge into the lower country, into the thick forest, and the wind began to blow harder.

How far had they come? Five, six miles? The days were short and darkness was not far off, and they had been traveling at least three hours.

"We're in for trouble, Tom." John Child was breaking trail and he had stopped abruptly and turned. "She's picking up to blow."

"No use to wear ourselves out," Radigan said. "We'll find a place to dig in."

They started on.

The wind was raw against their faces which grew stiff from cold, so numb it was difficult to speak, and the wind prevented hearing.

Suddenly John Child turned into the woods again and he stopped at the base of a huge deadfall. Here some great wind or other cause had uprooted a giant spruce and thrown it down with a mass of earth clinging to the root pattern. The roots and earth stood up in a solid wall seven or eight feet in diameter.

Without words, Radigan and Child moved into the forest and were busy with their knives, building a lean-to with the open face toward the root mass. The lean-to was covered with a thick thatching of spruce boughs, and inside a bed was made thick with other boughs. On the snow close to the root mass Radigan laid several heavy chunks of wood side by side on the snow to make a bed for the fire, then built a fire whose heat could be reflected by the root mass into the lean-to.

"Couldn't we have gone on?" Gretchen asked. "I mean, it's only a few miles farther."

"We'd still be sleeping in the cold, and by then we'd be more tired. When you travel in the cold, never exhaust yourself. Only exhausted people need freeze, believe me. If all travelers in the snow and cold would think of that, few of them would freeze. Just find some shelter or build some and curl up and sleep it out."

"But if you sleep, won't you freeze?"

"Not unless you're already exhausted. If all the heat inside your body is gone, used up in struggling, then you'll freeze, so just stop in plenty of time. I've slept out many a time when it was forty, fifty below."

The shelter was in a little hollow, and the still-falling snow added to the warmth by covering the spruce boughs with a thick cushion of snow. Wind whipped around the corner of the shelter into the space, so they built an added windbreak of spruce boughs.

They huddled over the fire and drank scalding coffee and chewed on jerked meat. Nobody felt like talking. Outside their shelter the wind whipped snow into the air and by the time they had finished their coffee it was blowing a gale. They had gone into camp none too soon.

Angelina Foley stood by the window of Radigan's ranch house and looked down the trail. She was frightened, and she was cold. But the cold was inside, not outside, for the room was warm and comfortable. The cold inside was the cold of fear, and of a kind of hatred such as she had never dreamed possible of herself.

Harvey Thorpe was at the table behind her, and across from him was Ross Wall. The big foreman had come in only minutes ago, and was sagging over the table, his face drawn with exhaustion. He had been lost most of the night, and his horse was dead—it had collapsed from exhaustion after bucking the deep snow for hours—and it was pure luck that Wall had found a cluster of trees and brush that offered partial shelter where he could build a fire. He had come into the ranch, staggering and falling. How he had lived through the blizzard of the night before he would never know, nor how he had gotten here. Fortunately, he could have been scarcely two miles from the ranch when he found his shelter, but he must have traveled twice the distance from the cave to the ranch to get here.

"He's dead then." Gelina heard the satisfaction in Harvey's voice and for some reason it angered her.

She turned on them. "I'll believe him dead when I see him dead."

"Don't be foolish." Harvey looked up at her, his pale blue eyes almost white in the reflection from the window. "Coker wanted to kill him, and he had his chance."

He got to his feet and crossed to the window. "All you have to do, Ross, is ranch—run the cattle and do the best you can. You'll have four men."

He looked up.

"And the rest?"

"I'll take care of them. You don't see anything. You don't know anything."

Ross turned the idea over in his mind, studying it

reluctantly. He needed no blueprints, and he should have guessed, knowing Thorpe as he did, and the crew he had around him.

"It's the wrong time," he said patiently. "It won't work, Harvey."

Thorpe smiled. He was feeling expansive. He tucked his thumbs in his vest pockets. "Ross, you've no imagination. This is one of the most remote ranches in the country, but a ranch where dozens of trails come down from the north, old Indian trails, no longer traveled, trails that can take a man quickly to Denver, Leadville, or a dozen other places.

"I tell you it's perfect! A quick move into one of those towns, or to a mining camp where they're shipping gold, then back here by a roundabout route, using the trails we know. I knew when I saw it this was the place, a legitimate ranch with no close neighbors, easy access to the places where gold is, and easy escape."

"It won't work," Ross insisted. "If what Miss Foley says is true, there's liable to be an investigation, anyway."

Thorpe shrugged. "Believe me, it's a *fait accompli* now, and nobody will be anxious to cause trouble for us. Radigan will have disappeared, and we are quiet, honest ranchers who pay our bills and preserve the peace. We'll keep ourselves clean around here, you see, and nobody will ever be the wiser."

"No."

They both turned at the sound of Angelina's voice, and Thorpe started to speak, but she interrupted.

"No, Harvey, we won't do it."

"You want to go to work in a saloon?" he asked mildly. "Or start a restaurant? That's all that's left."

She was silent. During the days of snow the herd had scattered and drifted, and without doubt many of them were dead, just as Radigan had warned her—he had been so right, and she hated him for it.

She hated him and now she hated Harvey, for now she saw how she had been duped, not that she hadn't agreed to much that had been done, including the theft

of cattle and the arrangements for the killing of the supposed squatter on the ranch they believed belonged to
them, but it was obvious now that from the first Harvey
had had his own plans and had acquiesced in hers only
to forward his own, and he had maneuvered her into a
position from which no escape seemed possible.

More than once she had suspected Harvey Thorpe's
activities during those absent years, and now she was
sure. But had she a choice? And after all, might it not
work? It was true there was money in the mining camps
of Colorado and Nevada, and it was true this was a
relatively foolproof hideaway. Anybody approaching
could be seen for some distance before arriving at the
ranch. Yes, it might work.

And mining the stages and the gold shipments was
quicker, easier, and scarcely more risky than ranching.

Radigan was dead. She had hated and feared him
but he was dead, and now she felt a curious emptiness,
a sense of loss.

It was an unfamiliar feeling, and it disturbed her,
for never before had she given much thought to anyone,
and in the case of Radigan, she herself had been first to
order his death. Yet now that he was dead she felt uncertain and lost, as if something she valued had gone
out of her life.

Standing by the window, listening to the talk behind
her, she sensed Wall's reluctance, and remembered what
she had often said to Harvey, that they must be careful
with Ross, for there was a point beyond which he would
not go. Now she was aware of that more keenly than
over, yet he said nothing, and if left to handle only the
honest work of handling cattle, he might stand aside
and remain quiet.

What about her? Somehow in the last few days control had slipped from her fingers, leaving Harvey in
command. He had taken the reins so quietly and skill-
fully that she was confused, for until now she had
despised him and been sure he would run her errands
for her, and listen to her. Now she knew she was mis-

taken, and she knew she did not like the thought. Something had to be done!

Yet, why do anything?

Why not sit back and let him engineer the robberies, and when there was enough to warrant it, find one man who would use a gun for her. And then San Francisco, New York, Paris, Vienna—and lots of money.

This way she was free. If they were caught, it was all his action. She had no idea . . . why, she was just ranching . . . Wall was her foreman, and see what they had done. Naturally, she could not control Harvey Thorpe. Yes, it would work, and just that way.

"Ross," she would begin now, "as soon as the storm is over, take two men and try to find an estimate of what we have left. Then we'll start building back."

When Ross Wall had gone she walked to the table and sat down. Harvey rolled his cigar in his teeth and smiled at her. He was feeling good, for now, after a long wait and a lot of submission to her will, he had won. From here on he was in the driver's seat, and he liked the feeling. Moreover, he could see that Angelina was aware of the shift of leadership. "On the fifth of next month," he said, "there is a shipment of gold leaving Leadville for Denver. It will never arrive."

The bullet smashed into the table between them and she heard the tinkle of glass. She stared at the deep furrow plowed into the wood of the table, shocked by its suddenness.

The second bullet shattered the lamp and spilled flame over the room, but Thorpe, acting swiftly, beat out the flames with a blanket before they had time to take hold.

They crouched near the floor in the darkness, frightened and breathing heavily, smelling the smoke, the spilled oil, and the singed wool of the blanket.

"You're so clever," Angelina said wickedly, "so very clever! He's still alive, Harvey, and you've failed again. *Radigan is alive!*"

Harvey Thorpe made no reply. Crouching in the darkness he was suddenly swept by a wave of blind, unreasoning fury. He wanted to leap out into the open, to kill, to cripple, to beat down. But the enemy was beyond him, somewhere out there, elusive in the dark.

"It can't be!" he protested. "It's somebody else! It simply can't be!"

"Your plans, they're so complete, Harvey. So thorough. I don't know how you do it."

"Shut up!" His tone was low and vicious, never before had she heard him sound so murderous. "He's dead, I tell you. It's that breed, or somebody."

Crouched in the darkness, waiting for further shots, she tried to examine her own position clearly. For the first time she realized that she felt active dislike for Harvey Thorpe. That she had not realized this before was due in part to their respective positions, for the ranch had been left to her, the cattle were in her name, everything was hers and she felt in no way obligated to him, while hers was definitely the superior position. Yet this move had been advised and instigated by him. It had seemed a good move, and she had been prepared for it, yet now she could see where she had played into his hands, and with the herd gone, or at least badly hurt by the storm, their positions were reversed. All this she had thought of earlier, but now she was wondering what her next move would be. That Ross Wall was loyal to her and to her alone, she knew. Also that their economic position was very bad: perhaps it would be better, if they eliminated the present danger, to go along with Harvey until he had acquired the gold, then take it for herself. She was sure she would never be suspected of conspiring with him to rob stages, and even if they suspected her, she naturally would have had no demonstrable hand in the robberies.

They waited in the darkness. Harvey sat with his back against the strong wall of the house in the direction from which the fire had come, and now he rolled a smoke in the dark, and lighted up.

"There's nothing he can do," Harvey said, finally. "He can't live out there in the cold forever—look what shape Ross was in—and we can bottle him up and keep him in this country until we can hunt him down."

"What if he knows of those Indian trails you talk of?"

"Mostly, they're snowed in now."

"Won't that affect your plans to get away after the holdups?"

He was silent for several minutes and then he said irritably, "No—we'll make provision for that."

Harvey Thorpe, she recalled, was a man who planned carefully, but did not like objections to his plans. He did not like to admit that he might be in error, and he was also an optimistic planner: he expected the breaks to go his way. This, she remembered having heard, was true of the criminal mind; few of them were ever willing to assess the full weight of the forces against them.

Yet he might win, for a time, at least. Getting to her feet she went into the other room and brought back a blanket which she hung over the window, and after that she lighted a candle taken from a box in the kitchen. With a broom she swept up the broken glass and threw it out, along with the ruined lamp.

When she returned to the living room Harvey had gone. Her thoughts returned to Tom Radigan.

Was he actually dead? The more she thought of that, the less she believed it. He was a shrewd fighter, one who missed few chances, and no matter how strongly Wall might believe him dead, she was unconvinced. Coker was not the man to kill Tom Radigan.

For several days nothing happened. The sun came out and melted the snow in exposed places, and Ross Wall, working tirelessly, checked their losses, and the reports he brought to her were not as bad as she had first expected. True, they had lost several hundred head, but it was mostly the weakest stock that would scarcely last out such a winter in any event. If the bad weather had remained they could have lost the entire herd, but now they had a respite.

The activities of the few riders Harvey had left her were limited by the snow-filled passes and trails blocked with snow. As most of her life had been spent in Western country she knew how difficult it was to search every corner of any range. And in this broken, tumbled and forested country it was virtually impossible. She had known of cowhands who had worked a range for years, and then discovered canyons they had never known to exist. Yet somewhere near Radigan had his own cattle and where they were there was feed.

Harvey was busy with his plans. He had divided the remaining force into three groups of six men each, and each had been given a project. Each group was to strike at the same time and then each was to get out of the country, fast. The country they were to cover was far to the north, but there were at least two ranches where they could get fresh horses, ranches owned by men who were themselves outlaws. Scouting north, they found the trails open as far as they rode, and there was a good chance they could make their strikes and escape before another snow fell.

Wall had been working with only four cowhands, and he came to Gelina as she was saddling for a ride. "I declare, Miss Gelina," he said, "we've covered a sight of country, but not one brand of his stock have we found, nor a single stack of hay."

"Maybe you've worked too close to the place," she suggested. "It must be a valley, or a plateau."

"We've been working west and south," he said, "but we'll try east and north, across the river."

She drew the girth tighter. "Ross, are there any tracks? Of people, I mean."

He hesitated. "I know what you mean," he said, after a moment, "but I've hesitated to say. Bitner found the tracks of the man who shot into the cabin."

She turned to face him, waiting. Yet even before he told her, she knew what was coming.

"It was Radigan, all right. He was on that pinnacle south of the place, although how he got there without being seen beats me. We found his tracks, and I know his tracks, and we backtrailed him to a camp in the hills a couple of miles over west. Mighty nice place, and they had a-plenty to eat."

"They?"

"Yes, ma'am. There was three of them. Radigan, John Child and the girl."

So Coker had failed after all? And what of Gorman?

Suddenly, she realized she was glad. She wanted Radigan alive. Yet was it that? Or was she pleased that Harvey had failed?

"Ross," she said, "you told me you'd found some grazing on a mesa over that way. I want you to cull what is left of the herd, and pick out about five hundred head of the best stock, and I want you to scout around and find the best grass you can, and get them on it."

He looked up at her, and she knew he understood exactly what she was thinking. "We may not be able to save them all," she said, "but I want to save enough to start again—elsewhere."

"All right." He shifted his feet and got out the makings, beginning to build a smoke. "I take it we're to make no talk about this?"

"No, no talk. Just do it."

"That Flynn," Wall said. "Harvey shouldn't think too little of him. He's no fool."

"Harvey's the fool." It was the first time she had let her feelings be known. "Radigan will beat him. Harvey's too reckless."

"I'll start working those cattle," Wall said. "You can depend on me."

That she could. She watched his broad back as he rode away and wondered who, if anyone else, she could depend on. Yet as he disappeared she was wondering if she would not do best to depend only on herself, and to keep her thoughts to herself. There might be a way to win out of this yet. If Radigan and Harvey destroyed each other, then she would remain in command of the situation.

And then Gorman showed up. He rode in on a gaunted horse, his face drawn and pale, his eyes fever-bright. She was alone on the ranch when he came in and she got the story first. It was brief and to the point, the story of Coker's death, and he added, "I found a deer in the deep snow and killed it. I've been eating meat without salt for the past three or four days, and not much of that."

After he had eaten and drunk coffee he rolled a smoke. "Ma'am, one thing I got to tell you. That Radigan! He wasn't worried. I mean not even a little. I never saw a man take things so easy-like, and I think there is reason for it. I think they knew exactly where they were going, and I think they went to Loma Coyote for help."

Gorman told her then what she had already heard from Ross, about the men at Loma Coyote, about Loren Pike, Charlie Cade and Adam Stark.

Tom Radigan rolled out of his blankets and stirred the few coals that remained from the night's fire. To these he added some fragments of bark and pitch pine he had split the previous evening. Shivering with cold, he moved swiftly to get the fire going, then dived back under his blankets. Glancing across, he saw Gretchen laughing at him from her bed.

"It's cold!" he said defensively.

"Naturally! But you should have seen yourself, jumping around like a cricket on a hot skillet."

"Tomorrow morning," he said grimly, "you build the fire!"

"All right! But I'll put the materials close by my bed so all I have to do is reach out with one hand and get the fire going."

"Anybody who'd make a fire like that," he said, "would steal sheep."

They waited, watching the hungry flames reach out with red tongues and caress the cold sticks. The fire grew and crackled, warming the cave on the mesa.

Actually, as to distance they were not more than a mile from the ranch itself, and the cave they occupied was one of a series atop the mesa that backed up the ranch, but they were on the northwest side of the mesa and the cave could only be entered from the top, so far as anyone knew. The room they occupied was a small one that was an offshot of a much larger room, and one that Radigan had prepared long ago.

His own preparations had only followed those of some other man who had preceded him by many years, for he had found an artificially hollowed basin there in the outer cave into which water flowed, and he had found a rusted halberd and part of a breastplate.

Here, sometime in the bygone years, some lost adventurer, perhaps from the army of Coronado, had taken a last refuge from the Indians. And from all the signs here he had lived for some time, years, perhaps. Cut off by the Indians, he must have fled ever farther into the wilds until finally at a last extremity he had found this place, and remained here. Gradually, over the years, he had fitted it out as a combination fortress and home.

Into the rock walls he had cut shelves, and in the outer wall he had cut two windows, or portholes, perhaps, that allowed him a means of covering the approach to the cave. And here he had lived.

Coming upon the place quite by accident, Radigan had immediately seen its value as a haven of refuge if the Utes caused trouble, and had supplied it with utensils, stored food and ammunition, and had, over the years, brought in a plentiful supply of firewood. The smokehole used by the previous occupant he had improved by a chimney from the crude fireplace, and the smoke issued from the top of the mesa through the roots and then the branches of a gnarled and ancient cedar. These served to dispel the smoke until it was scarcely visible a few yards away.

This was the first and best of the caches of supplies he had planted.

As the fire grew, the cave warmed up and Radigan rolled out of bed and dressed swiftly. Child followed.

"How about that trail north?" Radigan asked suddenly. "Figure a man could get through to Loma Coyote?"

"When do you want me to start?"

"Not you—me." Radigan walked to the deep-seat window and peered out. The approach to the cave was up a winding slide that was just short of being too steep for a horse to make it, and from below gave no hint of a means of access to the mesa's top. The window allowed a view down the slide for much of the distance. "You stay here, and I'll go," Radigan said.

"Those boys know me," Child protested.

"Pike knows me. So does Cade. The others can get acquainted. Anyway, it wouldn't do for me to stay here with Gretchen."

"Afraid?"

"Me?" Radigan stared at her, then grinned. "No, I'm not afraid, but you ought to be. There's no telling what might happen if we were left here alone."

"Nothing would happen," she replied, "unless I wanted it to."

Radigan measured her with cool eyes. "Now maybe that's so, and again maybe it isn't. Don't offer me any challenges."

He went into the outer cave where the horses were and fed them. He glanced at the hay—not much left, but there was a good bait of corn left, and there was a chance they could ride it out on what they had. There was food enough, that was sure. And ammunition enough to wage the Battle of Gettysburg all over again.

He saddled up, and went back for his blanket roll and saddlebags. Gretchen was up and had coffee on, and they sat down around the fire.

"About time somebody had a look at those cattle for San Antonio way," Child suggested. "I could do that."

Radigan looked over at Gretchen. "That means you'd be here alone. Could you make out?"

"I could." She added a slice of beef to his plate. "I would be all right, and if anybody found the place, I'd be able to stand them off."

"The snow's gone from the slide," Child said, "and

we can get out without leaving any trail, so you'll be all right. I can't figure any way they could find you up here."

When he had led the horse to the opening of the cave, Radigan walked back to meet Gretchen. He took the last packet of food she gave him and thrust it down in his saddlebags. "You be careful," she warned.

He turned and looked down at her. Somehow, despite the cold and discomfort of their days, she had continued to keep herself attractive, and now looking down into her eyes, he felt her concern. "You do the same," he said, "and don't you go out of the cave unless you go on top of the mesa, and if you do that, keep well back from the sides. And whatever you do, don't cook at night."

"You told me that. At night you can smell the food cooking."

"That's right. A wood fire don't matter so much because it could come from their own fireplace, but the smell of food is going to make them mighty curious."

"I won't."

He stepped into the saddle. Her fingers lingered on his sleeve. "You be careful," she repeated.

He glanced at her again, and was startled to see tears in her eyes. He looked hastily away. Now why would she be crying? There was no accounting for women, and it wasn't as if he was a relative or anything. He walked the horse the last few steps out of the cave and then started down the slide. It was steep, but a horse could make it. At the end he drew up and listened, but there was no sound.

He reached the bottom, glanced each way, then put his horse across the open and into the trees. He was visible for no more than two minutes and, once under cover of the pines, he turned in his saddle and watched John Child across the open. Then they both waited, unmoving, watching all around them for several minutes. Finally, Child said, "I guess we made it."

Radigan nodded. Reluctantly, he turned his horse and headed down through the trees. It was not right to leave a girl alone like that, alone for days on end, and probably scared. Although Gretchen was less afraid than any woman he had ever known . . . not one word of complaint through all of this, and never once when she shirked her work. In cold and snow, everywhere, she had held up her end of the work and the riding.

Where the Vache Creek trail met with the easy way to Valle San Antonio, they parted.

John Child looked twice his size in the heavy buffalo coat. He drew up, the steam from his breath making a plume in the still, cold air. "You be careful, Tom," Child said. "All those boys up there aren't friendly."

"All right."

"You watch especial for Swiss Jack Burns. He's a gunman from over Kansas way. Fancies himself."

"Yeah?" Radigan grinned. "With Loren Pike over there he's probably dead by now." He gathered his reins. "Loren, he never was much given to let be. Fact is, he's a right impatient man, sometimes."

Radigan picked out the broad shoulder of Cerro Jarocito to the north. East of there was a spring and it was only about six miles to that spring. Call it seven to be sure. Then three or four miles over to Coyote Creek and about six or seven miles north to Loma Coyote. It was a good eighteen miles, anyway you looked at it, and cold riding. Five or six hours if he was lucky, and no telling how much if he was not lucky.

He was riding a dapple gray, a good horse that would weigh all of twelve hundred pounds and one who knew how to travel in snow and over icy trails.

The wind was from the north, the sky was slate gray and promising snow, a promise Radigan did not want fulfilled. The trail had not been traveled since the storm, and at places the snow had crusted hard. By noon, when he should have had ten miles behind him he doubted if he had come more than six, for several times he had gone out of his way to skirt drifts of snow, and once had gotten himself tangled in a thick growth of lodgepole, and had to ride more than a mile to get out of it, and two more miles before he found his way back to the trail. He was swearing when he found it and the dapple was agreeing with him, shaking its head with disgust.

He had watered the horse at the spring, and when they reached Coyote Creek the water was frozen over at several places, which made crossing difficult, for the ice was not strong enough to bear the weight. The wind blew cold down the canyon from the north, stiffening Radigan's face and making his hands numb.

It was late dusk when he came down out of the canyon and rode across the bench and into the town.

The narrow street was as still as the day the earth was born, still and cold in the last light of day, with lights showing in the Ramble House, and across the street at the Utah Saloon. The only other light showed at an eating place, a light that showed from beyond a fly-specked window.

Loma Coyote was not much as towns went, and as towns went, Loma Coyote would someday go. It was a stopping place for drifters, a cooling-off place for men wanted by the law and who had found other places too hot for comfort. There was nothing going on at Loma Coyote that anybody could mention, a couple of miners who worked dismal prospect holes in the nearby mountains but did most of their drilling without a single-jack at the walnut bar of the Utah Saloon.

The population rarely exceeded thirty persons, all but three or four of them male. Once the population had leaped overnight to a surprising fifty-six, but that was during a Ute war when prospectors and trappers fled the hills for the doubtful security of Loma Coyote.

They were silent men, accustomed to loneliness, and the combination of too much company and too much of Loma Coyote's own brand of whisky had led to results somewhat less than surprising. By daybreak of the second day the population had decreased to fifty-three, and there were three bodies lying in an empty shed awaiting a spring thaw for burial.

By the sixth morning the population was almost back to normal, for one by one the newcomers decided the

Utes were less to be feared than the population and whisky of Loma Coyote.

At the far end of the street was a huge, drafty old structure that could only be a barn, and a lantern hung outside over a scarcely legible sign that indicated the premises were a livery stable.

In the front of the building was a dark little room in which a stove glowed cherry-red but there was no other light.

Out of the gloom a voice called. "Hay a-plenty, an' he'p yourself. Corn if you're a might to, but that'll be four-bits extry."

"That's a lot of money."

"Take it or leave it, but you stick your lunch-hooks into my corn bin without I say and you'll catch yourself a death of cold, because I'll open your belly with a shotgun."

The old man came out of the "office" carrying a sawed-off shotgun, and he held up a lantern, peering at Radigan. "Man can't be too careful, that's what I always say. You're *un*-titled to feed your hoss here, but them as wants corn I figure can pay for corn, because most likely they're running from something."

"I'm not running, old man. I'm looking for a friend of mine. His name is Loren Pike."

"Never heard of him. No memory for names. I figger names don't cut much ice, this here country. Man changes his name 'bout as often as he changes his address, and with most folks hereabout, that's mighty often."

"I own a ranch south of here. The name's Radigan."

He peered at Radigan again. "Maybe you own a ranch, maybe you don't, an' iffen you do, maybe you won't own it long. Not what I hear folks say."

"I own it, and a year from now, ten years from now I'll still own it." Radigan stripped the saddle from the dapple. "And if I have any trouble from you I'll ride back up here and burn this flea cage around your dirty ears."

The old man drew back. "Now what kind of talk is

that? Ain't I puttin' your hoss up for you? Didn't I say he'p yourself to corn? Didn't I?" The old man looked at him shrewdly. "Why, you might be the man John Child works for?"

"Child works for me."

"All right. I'll rub your horse down, and I'll give him a bait of corn. And if you're lookin' for any newcomer you might try the Utah or the Ramble. Most folks favor one or the other. On'y my advice to you is to get out of town. Sleep in the haymow if you're a might to, but stay shut of those places. Swiss Jack is full of trouble tonight."

Tom Radigan walked to the door, ducked his head against the cold wind and walked down to the eating house. He opened the door and stepped in, accompanied by a few blown flakes. A big, hard-faced woman stood behind the counter and shoved coffee over to him. "You can eat," she said, "but if you're lookin' for anything else, it ain't to be had. Not tonight, anyway."

"I want to eat."

She looked at him. "Yes, I reckon you would. Be an hour for you get any notions, I'd say, get the cold out of you then, and you'll be looking for something else. Takes a while for the cold to get out of a man's muscles. I've got three girls here, one sixteen and two nineteen, and I can handle more business than the three of them —and better."

"I'll settle for a thick steak."

"You'll take b'ar meat, an' like it. We ain't had any cow meat around here since the storm. Fellers drive it up from the south of here, but the trails are closed."

Radigan ate in silence while the big woman talked on, apparently neither listening to his occasional comments or caring if he listened to her stream of conversation.

When he had eaten he tossed a dollar on the counter and she handed him three quarters in change. He took a last gulp of scalding coffee and got up, shoving out into the cold. "Don't you come the high and mighty on me!" she called after him. "You'll be back!"

He crossed the street, following a beaten path, to the Utah Saloon.

It was a bar no more than ten feet long and of hand-hewn planks, and the man behind it was nearly as tall as the bar was long. Two men leaned on the bar and several others sat around at tables. They all looked up when he came in, and, seeing he was a stranger, looked again.

"Whisky," he said, "or whatever you serve by that name."

The big man leaned over the bar. "You don't like our drinkin'? Then you can do without."

"Give it to me. I don't know whether I like it or not."

"You'll decide or you won't get it."

"All right! I like it." Radigan glanced around at the others. They returned his gaze solemnly, and he said, "If these gentlemen like the whisky, I'll buy."

The big bartender turned again. "Now see here, stranger. That's again you've throwed a doubt on my liquor. I don't like it."

"See?" Radigan grinned at the others. "He admits he doesn't like it himself."

The big man interrupted angrily. "I said no such thing. I meant—"

"Trying to weasel out of it," Radigan said. "Well, fill a glass and I'll see if I like it."

The big man stared at him for an instant, then went behind the bar and poured a drink. Nobody else moved. "The offer stands," Radigan invited.

Nobody moved.

"See? Nobody likes it."

He tasted it. For an instant he thought his throat was on fire, then he backed off and looked at the glass. "A barrel of branch water, two plugs of tobacco, a bar of soap to give it a bead, and a couple of ounces of strychnine, and maybe three gallons of alcohol. Color the whole thing with greasewood, and that's about the formula. No wonder nobody drinks it."

He tasted it again. "Started by selling to the Utes,

I'll bet. No wonder they went on the warpath so much."

"You're breedin' trouble," the big man warned.

"No I'm not, and I don't want trouble. Now you haul out that jug from under the bar and I'll have a decent drink."

The bartender muttered gloomily and reached under the bar. Immediately the others got up and walked over to join Radigan.

When the glasses were set up and the drinks poured, Radigan said, "I'm Radigan of the R-Bar outfit. You should know the brand. You've eaten R-Bar beef, time to time."

A round-faced man with a sour face looked at the whisky in his glass, then tossed off half of it. "You accusin' us of rustlin'?"

"Stating a fact," Radigan said. "And I'm not the man to begrudge a beef now and again, although why you waste time on my little herd when there's nearly three thousand head in the country that don't belong there."

"You invitin' us?"

"Telling you. What you do is your own affair, only they're no friends of mine. Fact is, I'm right in the middle of a first-class cow war."

The door opened behind them and in a gust of cold wind a slender blond man came in. He was tall, wiry, and his face was narrow with straight brows above long, deep-set eyes. He wore a short sheepskin coat that gave his gun hand plenty of room and a round beaver cap that fitted his narrow skull tightly.

At the same moment there was a clatter of horses' hoofs in the outer street, and Radigan glanced out the window. In the narrow shaft of light he saw Harvey Thorpe, and the men around him were Thorpe's men.

Radigan tossed off his drink and shrugged into his coat. The newcomer was watching him. "I don't know you," he was saying. "I'm Swiss Jack."

Radigan grinned at him. "My name is Will Hafto-wate. And that's what you'll have to do."

"What?" Swiss Jack looked inquiringly.

"You'll have to wait," Radigan said. "I spoke of a cattle war: that's it, out front."

Swiss Jack glanced over his shoulder. The group of riders were dismounting outside. "That's no cattle war. That's Bob Harvey, and if he wants to see you, I'm going to keep you for him."

"Let him alone." The big bartender had leaned across the bar. "We don't hold anybody for anybody here."

"Now, see here——"

The back door closed softly, and Swiss Jack turned sharply around. Radigan was gone.

six

The wind blew cold off the mountain as Radigan paused on the icy back step, listening for sounds within. He could hear the murmur of voices but could distinguish no words, and he waited only until he heard the front door open and then he walked swiftly along the well-beaten path to the outhouse and went past it to the barn.

He paused there, his shadow merging with the heavier shadow alongside the barn wall, and he calculated swiftly. There were only a few buildings in town and all would be searched at once, therefore shelter within any of them was out of the question.

The arrival of Thorpe and his riders was a puzzle, for it was impossible they could have known of his coming here. They might be looking for Pike and Cade, but that was doubtful as thus far they had no argument with them. Hence it was logical to assume they had come here for some other reason and their arrival at this time was purely coincidental. But why would they come here?

And Thorpe had at least a dozen riders with him, and perhaps even more.

Swiss Jack had called him Bob Harvey. Was that a mistake? Or another name Thorpe had used? Radigan recalled his own first impression, that Thorpe was a tough man, one who had been known somewhere before this. But Bob Harvey? He turned the name over in his mind, but it meant nothing to him.

No use standing where he was. He went around the corner of the barn his feet crunching on the frozen snow under the eaves. Back of the barn, and perhaps thirty yards off was the creek bed. He started for it, moving swiftly, not wanting to be caught outlined against the snow, and when he reached the blackness he stopped to catch his breath and to listen.

The back door had slammed. Was the search starting? If there was a search he was sure it would be Swiss Jack who started it: the others, whatever else they might be were men who kept their own counsel.

He moved back into the brush along the creek, then went down along the icy rocks. His Winchester was with his saddle and gear back in the livery stable, but to go for it now was fatal.

He saw men fanning out from the barn, going from building to building. Obviously, the idea that he might have remained outside on such a cold night had not occurred to them, but it would soon come to mind. Yet only a few minutes had passed when he heard a call. It was Thorpe's voice. "All right! No time for that! Come on in! We'll take care of him on the way back!"

The way back from where?

He saw them straggle back and mount up, and then they rode out of town in a tight cavalcade as if bunching against the cold.

If men traveled on such a night there, haste was imperative and they must have far to go.

Nobody commented when he came back into the saloon and this time the bartender reached under the bar for the good jug and poured a drink, "On the house," he said.

"Cold out there," Radigan commented.

"Especially," it was Swiss Jack, "if you have cold feet to begin."

Radigan took his drink and his time. Then he turned slowly around and looked at Swiss Jack. He looked at him for a full minute while the room was silent. The fire crackled and inside the pot-bellied stove a stick fell. A man shifted his feet and poured a glass full and the trickling of the whisky could be heard plainly in the room.

"Yes," Radigan said quietly, "I had cold feet from a long ride, and cold hands, and there were a few more outside than I was in any mood to tackle. There must have been a dozen of them."

"So?" Swiss Jack was sitting back in his chair, smiling.

"There's only one of you."

Swiss Jack was surprised. He had expected everything but that and for an instant it caught him unawares, and also, he instantly realized, he was in no position to draw a gun and any slightest move on his part could be construed as a move to draw. If the big man at the bar was any hand at all with a gun, then Swiss Jack himself was as good as dead. And he was not ready to die.

For a long moment he sat very still, wondering if he dared move from his slouched position without feeling the tear of hot lead in his guts.

Radigan knew exactly how Swiss Jack was feeling and he was in no hurry to let him off the hook. "I said just any time," he said, "but if you reach for a gun, I'll kill you."

Swiss Jack's mouth was dry and he could feel his pulse throbbing heavily. He dearly wanted to move, his position had become cramped, but he was quite sure now that the big man was not fooling.

Radigan watched him, his eyes cold but his lips smiling slightly. He did not want to kill this man, yet he knew that if it became necessary he was not going to lose any time doing it or any sleep afterwards. He did not want to brag but he knew that sometimes even a dangerous man will hesitate before tackling an equally dangerous one.

"You called that man Bob Harvey. I don't know the name."

"Your hard luck."

"Not mine. He's yellow enough to hire his killing."

Swiss Jack laughed. "Bob *Harvey?* You've the wrong man. Bob can kill his own cats."

"He hired Vin Cable to kill me."

He saw the sudden awareness in Swiss Jack's eyes and knew now that whatever else Swiss Jack might do he was not going to begin a fight under any misapprehensions.

"You're Radigan?" There was a slight note of incredulity.

"I'm Radigan."

By now he knew the story of the killing of Vin Cable would be known wherever Western men gathered, for such stories were quickly passed on from campfire to card table across the country. And especially were such stories the gossip of such places as this, where they were meat and drink to the lonely men who lived by the gun.

The door opened then and three men came into the room. The first was a tall, square-shouldered man with auburn mustaches and auburn hair that touched his shoulders. The second was shorter, a man with a square face and a square build who carried himself very erect, a man whose features were swarthy and handsome in a hard-bitten way. The third was even taller, very narrow across his rounded shoulders and with a small head atop a long neck, and a great beak of a nose.

Radigan said, "Howdy, boys." He did not remove his eyes from Swiss Jack. "I'm selling tickets for a ball. You boys want to choose your partners?"

"If it's your fight, Tom," Loren Pike had grasped the situation at once, "we're already tuning our fiddles."

Charlie Cade and Adam Stark walked around Radigan to the bar and leaned their backs against it, looking at Swiss Jack.

"You really call this a fight?" Pike asked gently, indicating Swiss Jack.

"This is the soup. The main course is being served when Harvey Thorpe or Bob Harvey or whatever he calls himself comes back down the trail."

Swiss Jack was getting stiff. He knew he was going to try moving soon, and he was glad there was only one man to reckon with for the men who stood before him were all very tough men.

Radigan walked slowly over to the table. "Your hands aren't tied, Jack," he said conversationally, "and

I think you said something about holding me for Harvey. You want to make a start?"

Swiss Jack was looking up, his eyes on Radigan's chest. If he did draw, would his gun clear the table? Could he jerk free of the table and get his gun up before he died?

"Seems to me you're in a bind," Radigan said. "Just get up out of the chair. You'll get an even break. Just get up mighty easy and don't make any sudden moves."

Swiss Jack could not make himself believe it. He was going to have his chance. Slowly, he eased sideways out of his chair and straightened up and his eyes lifted to Radigan's and Radigan hit him.

Swiss Jack never saw the blow coming. He was not set to take a punch and he was not yet on balance. The blow caught him alongside the jaw and lights exploded in his skull and the next instant he was seated on the floor and his skull was ringing. There was a smoky taste in his mouth and he started to get up but a big hand caught him by the scuff of the neck and slammed him back into the wall with such violence that a bottle on the bar tipped over. His skull hit the wall with a vicious rap and his eyes tried to focus and he tried to reach for a gun.

He had never been in a fist fight in his life. Guns were a gentleman's weapon, and he had always relied on a gun. A hard fist caught him in the mouth and he tasted blood. He came off the wall swinging, but a wicked blow in his belly took his wind and doubled him up for the lifting knee that broke his nose.

"Swiss Jack," Radigan spoke without anger, "I came in here a stranger, minding my own affairs, and you decided to take a hand.

"Now," Radigan continued, "I'd suggest you settle down for the winter here, or you ride out to the north. But don't come south of here because if I see you south of Loma Coyote and west of Santa Fe I'll take it to mean you're looking for me."

He turned and walked to the bar. "I need some top hands," he said to Loren, "who aren't gun-shy."

Gretchen spent the first day cleaning up the cave, checking the trail regularly, and during that first day she cooked not at all, only making coffee to go with the jerked beef and the cans of tomatoes she opened. She was, she admitted to herself, frightened.

On the second day the wind was blowing hard into the west, and so away from the ranch, and on that day she got out some dried apples and baked three apple pies. She had already decided on a party for them when they returned, and she had begun preparing.

What she did not know was that Bitner, scouting wide for the R-Bar cows, had swung even farther west than usual on what was to be the last venture in that direction before they started sweeping the mountains to the east of Vache Creek. And returning from that ride he caught a whiff of fresh baking.

It was impossible, he knew it was impossible, yet he knew that smell, and his stomach growled in response. He drew up and sat his horse in the face of the wind, trying to get another whiff of it, but none came. Just as he was deciding it was all imagination and wishful thinking, it came again.

For an hour he cut back and forth across the wind, trying to trace that vagrant aroma, but without success, although he did catch the scent several times, and by that time he was closer to the ranch by several miles.

When it was almost dusk he gave it up. It was nonsense. Probably they were baking at the ranch, and even if Radigan was holed up out here somewhere, they would hardly be baking pies or cake. Although, come to think of it, there had been some doughnuts left in a pan when they took over the ranch.

They had turned the barn into a bunkhouse and there were several men there when he rode in. After a few minutes he went up to the house to report to Ross Wall, who was talking to Angelina Foley.

When he opened the door he expected the odor of fresh baking to hit him with a wave, but it did not.

His nostrils found no expected odors there, nothing but that of a wood fire and fresh coffee.

Bitner was a cautious man, and after a moment he merely reported what he had seen and found, which was nothing but empty country. He kept the smell of baking to himself. After all, it was probably his imagination.

The cattle were in bad shape. The grass they had found was eaten down to the grass roots and the cattle were not used to pawing snow away from grass to eat it and were poor rustlers. That Wall was worried, he could plainly see, and Miss Foley's face looked drawn and worried.

And then a man rode in from Loma Coyote with the news that Radigan had been seen there, and Gorman told him while they were having a smoke, "I saw tracks over east of here, I'd swear they were the tracks of that big roan that the halfbreed rides."

"Fresh?"

"Yesterday or the day before. And if he went he's still out there. I cut for sign all the way back and up and down along the creek. He hasn't crossed back."

Suppose, Bitner told himself, they have a hideout near the ranch? And suppose both men are gone? Then that girl will be there alone.

The girl alone.

She was a lot of woman, that one. Bitner's narrow eyes closed over his thoughts. He was no chaser, but when a man was away from women for months he got to feeling it.

Bitner was out at daybreak and he rode west along a faint trail with the mesa towering over him on his right, and he had no idea in mind except to find where that smell of baking had come from. Not that the girl was not in the back of his mind, clinging there like some noxious vine, working its feelers into his thoughts with memories of the girl, her high-breasted figure and the way she walked.

Damn! That was a woman! And living with two men like that! No decent girl would think of it. Claimed

Child was her father! Why, that breed couldn't father a blonde like that out of—anything. Bitner knew what trouble could come to a man from fooling around with a woman in the West. He knew it, but he was not thinking about it. He knew a man could steal cows, commit a murder and even steal a horse and get away with it, but to fool around with a woman, especially a decent woman. The least he could get was a hanging.

He knew all that but he could not get the girl out of his thoughts. She was there, like a cocklebur in a horse's tail, and nothing was going to get it out in any easy way.

He walked his horse along the slope, working his way west, and thinking it out. If they had a hideout close to the ranch the chances were it was somewhere around that mesa. It loomed up there, hundreds of feet above them, and no man could see what was on top, and so obvious nobody would ever think of looking there.

Radigan, he was a cagey one. Thorpe should have measured his man more carefully before trying to move in as he had, but Bitner, being no fool, could see a lot of things Thorpe had not considered. There was a good chance he would never get back from this trip, and as far as that went, that Foley girl was mighty handsome . . . do her good, too. She was too high and mighty and too free with the orders to suit him. Bitner took a hefty bite from his chewing tobacco and rolled it into a corner of his jaws. Do her good, that's what it would, but alongside this Child woman she was nothing. No wonder Radigan wouldn't fall for the Foley girl. Bitner knew about that, for he had seen the gleam in her eye when she went after him. She made like she was an enemy, but if Radigan so much as showed a sign of interest she was ready.

The dim trail, ancient as time itself, played out somewhere near the mesa, but trending away from the wall. Bitner drew up and spat a blob of brown juice into the remains of a snowdrift. He tested the air for the smell of cooking but found nothing but good, clean pine forest. He sat his horse, waiting patiently, for Bitner was a man who knew patience.

He worked at it the rest of the day and came in at night without saying anything except that he had been hunting. He was tired and so was his horse, and knowing the man for a top hand, Wall asked no questions.

Half the night Bitner lay awake thinking of Gretchen Child, and turning over in his mind every possible approach with the slow patience of the confirmed hunter. Nobody, he remembered, had examined that mesa, and certainly nobody had ridden around it, and it was a good long ride and one he decided to make. After all, he might be in this country a good while and he might as well get acquainted. He settled down into his worn blankets and slept, and far to the north a small column of riders was filing into place beside the road where they would camp, and their goal was not far off.

Harvey Thorpe was feeling good. Suppose they had missed Radigan. The man was on the dodge now and eventually they would kill him or run him out. A few more miles of riding and they would be in position to make their strike: the word he had from Leadville was that the stage might carry seventy thousand in gold. It was better than the cattle business.

Sure, he would come out of it with a third, but it was enough for now. And he might do a lot of things with a fast count; he had handled a lot of money and knew how to make a count look better than it was.

Radigan was beat. The long ride atop the other rides and he was tired. He holed up at Loma Coyote to wait out the weather a little, and to recuperate. John Child would be back at the hideout on the mesa by this night, and he was not worried.

The trouble was, John Child was lying unconscious beside the trail twelve miles east of the ranch where he had been thrown when his horse was startled by a sudden flushing of birds from the brush. Child had been tired, too, riding half-asleep in the saddle, and now he was out cold and had been for an hour. And his horse was just slowing to a walk, a couple of miles farther on.

Gretchen awakened on her third morning alone with a distinct feeling of uneasiness. She dressed hurriedly and went to the window and peered out. She could see nothing. Her range of vision was better from one of the inner windows, which was, like the first, concealed by a break in the rock, so she went back into the cave and looked out. And she saw a rider.

He was not passing by, he was cutting for sign, and he was working the ground as carefully as an Apache. Gretchen had not grown up with Indians not to know when a man was hunting a trail and close to what he wanted to find. She watched him, frightened and fascinated. Yet her first thought was for John Child and Radigan. What if they returned and he saw them first?

She went back into the cave and fed the horses. She got a pistol and belted it on, then picked up a rifle. She was a good shot, and if she got the chance: she had no occasion to kill any man, but this one was a danger to those she loved. When everything was arranged she went to the entrance and looked down. No sign of him there.

Radigan had showed her a rock she could push down. It might not kill a man but it could give him some uncomfortable moments and might make him think again before he tried to come up the slide a second time. She tested that and it moved under her hand. Yes, she could roll it. She checked the windows, and the man was no longer in sight. That frightened her more than ever, because not being able to see where he was she could imagine all sorts of things. And the worst of it was, Radigan and her father were due back at any moment.

She looked out again, and saw the man farther down the slope, working through the trees. Had he failed to find any tracks? Or was he aware he was being watched? Suppose he waited until dark and then came up?

The day wore on slowly, and she went ahead with her plans for the party she had promised herself she would provide for their homecoming. Into her small pack she had hidden one very nice dress. It was right for a party, and she got it out hoping some of the wrinkles would hang out. She hung it up and looked at it, then went back to the window. There was no sign of the man.

Taking the rifle she went up to the top of the mesa and worked her way close to the edge, keeping off the skyline. He was there, riding back toward the ranch and some distance off. That did not mean he could not come back.

Gretchen had never thought of herself as brave or lacking in bravery. As a child she knew the Indians had thought her courageous. But bravery, she realized, was not a simple thing. Anyone could be brave under familiar circumstances, but put that same person in a strange place, among strange people and subjected to a different brand of fear and he might not be so brave. Many a man who was afraid of high places could walk into gunfire without hesitation, and a man who might ride any dangerous, man-killing horse might hesitate to rush into a fire to save someone. Usually a man was brave in a situation where he understood the risks, and what she thought of now was not in her estimation a matter of bravery or lack of it. She had a job to do and she decided she would do it.

If that man returned she must stalk and kill him. She could not run the risk of him lying in wait for Radigan and her father.

She covered several miles along the other side of the mesa, staring off into the gathering dusk, looking into the trees and over the bare hillsides, hoping they would return. She returned to the cave and built a small fire to make coffee, and she knew she was afraid.

It was very dark in the cave. The only comfortable feeling was the sound of the horses chomping on their grain in the stalls in the main cave.

She took straw from the pile near the horses and scattered some of it in the opening, hoping the rustle of it would arouse her if anyone walked over it. Farther inside she placed several little rows of stones that a man might kick in walking, and these would rattle on the bare floor of the cave. Yet she was frightened, and she lay awake for long hours, listening into the dark.

At daybreak she awakened suddenly, conscious that she had overslept. For a long time she lay absolutely still, listening, straining her ears for the slightest sound, and heard nothing. She got quickly to her feet and, taking the rifle, went to the windows, then the cave opening. There was nothing, no one in sight anywhere. Perhaps she was being foolish, the man might have lost something or— But she knew she was not. She knew the man had been looking for her, for them.

She made coffee and ate more of the jerked beef and some cold corn bread, and at intervals she went to look and saw nothing. She fed the horse only a little for the hay was all but gone and the corn was precious.

Her dress was hanging out surprisingly well and she longed to put it on. She had planned to wear it when they arrived and she was sure that would be soon. Again she checked the openings, but nothing was in sight. Taking her rifle she went to the top of the mesa and worked close to the edge, but there, too, she saw nothing.

From the other side of the mesa she studied the country to the north from which either Radigan or her father must come, but she saw nothing. She was sure once, that she did, but then there was no further movement so she gave up and went back.

Suppose they never came back? Suppose both of them had been ambushed and killed? Suppose once more she was to be an orphan with no one to turn to, no place to go, and no money?

She shook her head, refusing to accept the idea, and then she went back to the cave, and suddenly determined, she changed into her dress. Excitedly, she looked in the small mirror she had but could see only a little of herself at a time. She had put her hair up the night before, but now she let it down and combed it out.

When her hair was put up properly she looked at herself in the mirror and knew she was beautiful, and it was the way she wished to look when Tom Radigan returned home. The dress was white, with only a little color.

"I . . . I look like a bride!" she said aloud.

The voice came from behind her: "You sure do, lady!"

Suddenly she was cold, utterly cold. For a long moment she did not move, her mind working swiftly and with astonishing clarity. She knew she was in dire trouble and there was no help to be expected unless— unless—but their coming now was too much to hope for.

She turned slowly to see Bitner standing in the opening from the larger cave, and she recognized him at once. His face and name were familiar for when she arrived on the stage she had seen him and heard him called by name.

He was a lean, tall, sour-smelling man, unshaven and dirty, the juice from his tobacco staining the whiskers about his mouth.

"I was wondering when you'd get here," she said. "You certainly took long enough."

Bitner blinked. He had expected fear, screams, protests, anything but her present calm. And her appearance. Her very beauty left him awkward and uncertain as to his next move, for he was unused to women of such beauty and they robbed him of self-possession. But her shoulders were very white, and he stared at her, his mouth growing dry with eagerness. At the same time her attitude and appearance confused him and the fact left him angry. She was only a girl, and she was alone.

"I'm here now," he said crossly, "and I guess you know what I've come for."

"I saw you searching for the trail," she said. "I've watched you for several days. I could," she looked at him steadily, "have killed you."

He looked at her, disturbed by her coolness and the

uncomfortable feeling that he might have been, for days, right under her rifle.

"Won't do you no good," he said. "You missed your chance."

"I was making some coffee," Gretchen replied. "Would you like some?"

Every delay was a victory, every moment she could keep him talking increased her chances of something happening, of some opportunity, some chance to do something, anything. But whatever she did must be right the first time: there would be no second.

"Well . . . I could do with some coffee," he agreed.

Why not? Warm him up. It was mighty cold out there. He glanced around with new respect for Radigan. Had it mighty nice up here. Plenty of grub, warm shelter, feed for the horses and firewood; why, he could last out the winter here.

She walked right by him. She would never have believed, a moment before, that she could walk so close to him, but although her flesh crawled with fear, she did it.

"Pretty fancy," Bitner said, indicating the dress. "You wear that in some dance hall?"

"It is a party dress, Mr. Bitner," she said. "I wore it at parties in Mexico. I attended a convent there."

He accepted the coffee. "You," he was incredulous, "in a convent?"

"Why not?" she looked around at him. "I am seventeen, Mr. Bitner, and although you seem to doubt it, I am a lady."

He sneered, yet he felt a rising doubt. "Likely story! Livin' with two men!"

"John Child is my foster father. He and his wife were the only parents I ever had." She had located the bowie knife they used to slice meat. "He is a very good man, and Mr. Radigan has been nothing but a gentleman."

Bitner stared at her sourly. This was not going as he had planned, but somehow the right moment had not come. Meanwhile a cup of coffee would taste mighty good. He peered at her, trying to make out whether she was like she said, or like he had suspected. His opinion of her was convinced, however, and he decided she must be lying.

She stirred the coals under the coffee and got out two cups. The knife was just visible under the edge of an old coat she had used when she first got up in the morning, and she purposely avoided the area, not wishing to attract attention to it that might lead him to discover the knife. Bitner had seated himself close to her guns, which were useless under the circumstances.

When she handed him the cup he touched her hand with his and grinned at her meaningly. Gretchen seemed not to notice but inwardly she cringed.

"Ain't nobody comin' back here," Bitner said suddenly. "If you're expectin' it, you're wrong. We ain't seen nothing of Radigan since he rode north."

They knew that, then?

"He won't live long up there. Not with Swiss Jack Burns around. And if he does the boss will take care of him on the way back."

"He's been away?"

"He's away all right." Bitner gulped the hot coffee and muttered a little, looking around the cave at the few sparse articles of clothing and the beds. "That breed is good as dead, too." He puckered his brow. "We don't know what happened to him, but he's afoot out there in the cold, and he's hurt. We found blood on the snow and his horse came in to the ranch, so we back-trailed the horse. No sign of Child, but blood on the snow."

Sardonic humor glinted in his hard eyes. "No use gettin' your hopes up. Nobody ain't going to come to help you out." He crossed one leg over the other. "Best thing you can do is make up to me. A woman can't live in this country without a man."

She dropped her hand to the haft of the bowie knife and swung it in a wide arc. It was her chance and he was warm, relaxed, momentarily off guard. She swung the wide blade and turned with it, swinging it

amost at arm's length, and she was just short. The tip
of the blade slashed across his biceps and he dropped
the cup and toppled over backwards as the blade slit
his shirt and left a long, red scratch across his abdomen.
Instantly, Gretchen knew she had failed, and that now
there would be no respite, no further chance at delay,
and she had no doubt that after he had stayed with
her as much as he wanted that he would kill her: he
must kill her.

Gretchen did not think, she ran. But as she ran she
caught up her rifle and ran into the outer cave, then
scrambled on up the slide to the top of the mesa. The
wind was piercing, but she ran. She ran wildly, desperately, conscious of the clambering, stumbling footsteps of the man behind her.

Yet almost at once she was out of sight among the
scattered piñons.

She had not lived among Indians for nothing, and
quickly she fell to the ground among some scattered
rocks and low brush, and she lay still, the rifle for-
gotten in one hand, the knife in the other.

She had failed, and now he would hunt her down.
She had drawn blood, and the cut across his biceps
might be deep, and if it was he would not devote much
time to a search until he had done something to treat
the wound. And after that he would come for her.

She checked the rifle. There was a shell in the chamber and three more in the magazine: four shots.

It was not enough.

She was not that good a shot, and unless she let him
come close she would probably miss, and she could
not afford to miss often.

Yet, a moment later when she saw him moving some
distance off, she tried her first shot. It was a warning, to
remind him she had the rifle, and he dropped from
sight among some rocks, and being Indian in that
part of her thinking at least, she moved at once. She
retreated to a safer shelter, farther back on the mesa,
and settled down there to wait for whatever move

Bitner might make, and for a time he made none at all.

The day was drawing on and the air was cold. With night it would be piercing cold and windy atop the mesa and she dared not have a fire, nor was there any shelter she could find, nor a blanket anywhere.

She knew then it was well she had been an Indian, if only for a few years, for an Indian knows how to endure without crying to the sky, he knows how to withstand cold, hunger and the wind, and she would withstand them.

She knew then the dress she had on was the last thing she should be wearing; it was white, and too easy to see on the mesa's top, or anywhere. But it was a woman's dress, a dress for a woman to wear to meet her man, the last feminine thing she owned, and she was going to live with it or die with it, but dressed as a woman should be.

Gretchen remembered the cabin under the mesa and the warm fire, she remembered listening for Tom Radigan's step, and knew she was in love with him, knew it deep in every throbbing corpuscle, knew it in her muscles and bones and in the crying need of her body, her loins yearning for the man he was. And she knew then she was not going to die alone on the mesa top, she was not going to be killed and raped by such as Bitner. She belonged in her heart to Radigan, and she would belong to him in the flesh or to no man. She was not going to save that last bullet for herself, she was going to save it for him, for Bitner, and she was going to give it to him, right in the belly at point-blank range.

She had never felt like this before, but right now she was backed up against death with all the non-sense and the fancy words trimmed away. The hide of truth was peeled back to expose the bare, quivering raw flesh of itself, and there was no nonsense about it. She had been taught the way a lady should live, and how a lady should act, and it was all good and right and true and the way a pretty girl should be taught, but out here on the mesa top with a man hunting her to put her back on the grass it was no longer the same. Save the manners for the parlor and the ball room, and save the womanly tricks for courting, but this was something else and there was no fooling about it. She was going to kill a man and when he died she was not going to be sorry.

There are times in life when the fancy words and pretty actions don't count for much, when it's blood and dust and death and a cold wind blowing and a gun in the hand and you know suddenly you're just an animal with guts and blood that wants to live, love and mate, and die in your own good time.

Gretchen Child had the feel of the Indian in her, and she settled down behind the rocks and brush partly sheltered from the raw cold wind off the snow peaks, and she waited there, as ready to kill as any trapped lioness, and almost eager for it.

She was only a few months from a convent and a graceful house where ladies were gentle, fragile and delicate, but there was none of that here. She only knew in her guts that she wanted to live and that out there over those snow-dressed mountains her man was coming nearer, and she wanted to be waiting for him as a woman should.

Suddenly something fierce and wild came up in her and she jacked a shell into the chamber and made the sound ring, and then she called out, hoarse and wild, "Come on, Bitner! You want a woman, so come and get me, and if I don't kill you, Radigan will!"

Bitner, two hundred yards off, caught her voice coming downwind, and settled down behind his rocks, not liking the sound of it. He heard the sound of the Winchester, too, and said to himself, "Why, she's crazy! She's gone loco!"

But the need for her was in him and he settled down to see what a cold night on the mesa could do.

She was dressed flimsy, with shoulders bare to the wind, and not much body to the cloth in her dress. Right now she was full of beans, but a cold night might do a lot to her, and he could wait. He had waited this long.

Tom Radigan had come out of the trees to the north of the mesa, riding with the wind at his back and his eyes busy, sure he had heard a shot, although the wind was away from him.

To the east a few miles Charlie Cade, Loren Pike and Adam Stark were flanking it down through the trees in a thin skirmish line, hunting for Foley riders and studying out the country. Come hell or snow blowing there was going to be a fight before the sun lifted to noon tomorrow, and Radigan had an idea there'd be blood on the mountains before Pike, Cade and Stark turned tail.

He circled warily to the west, not liking the faint sound that had seemed to be a shot. The day was far along, but light enough for clear seeing, and once he thought he'd glimpsed something white on the rim. Two hours later he had circled and was coming up on the south side, and there he found tracks in the snow, searching tracks of a horseman cutting for sign.

There was a cold feeling in him then, and he turned the black horse he was now riding and started up the slope toward the mesa, and he rode right out in the open. He rode up to the steep rock slide and drew up, not liking the thought of bracing that slide with God knows what at the top.

Once he thought he heard a voice cry out in the late afternoon, but the sound whipped away and he knew he must be mistaken. Everything seemed all right. He could see the edge of the boulder placed for rolling down, sitting right where he'd left it. He stepped back and sat down to pull off his boots, and then slipped his feet into the Blackfoot moccasins he always carried for woods work, and then he took his rifle and started up the slide.

He had taken only one step when he heard the shot. It came clear on the wind, but caught by echoes and slapped around among the rocks. A shot right enough, and from somewhere above, but somewhere. There was no pinning down the sound.

He put out a moccasined foot and tested the rock, then swung his weight up. He wanted no rattling stones to warn of his coming, no sound, anywhere.

On top of the mesa Bitner chewed at the ends of his mustache and grinned into the wind. The little fool had grabbed a rifle and it was his she had taken, not her own, and he knew how many cartridges were left. It was a thing a man always knew, if he wanted to stay alive.

That last shot was number three. One bullet left. She had tried to get him, and once she had been close. He had taken a chance this last time, allowing her to see him plain enough to make her eager. He knew she was not too good with a rifle, although she could shoot. And she shot a split second too late and missed by a narrow margin, but enough. He milked the rifle down to one shot, and he had an idea he was going to have to gamble on that one if he wanted the woman, and he did, more than ever now.

It would be a fight, but he liked his women full of fight. He bit off another chew and thought about it, taking his time And she was a lot to think about. The wind blew cold, moaning around the evergreens and stirring icy snow around the rock where he sat.

Bitner rolled the tobacco in his jaws and decided she was a pretty canny woman. Small chance of her trying her last shot at a distance, so he could get close without too much risk. And when he got close he'd have to get hold of that rifle or chance a shot of his own to get the rifle away from her.

He moved out from the rocks and ran twenty feet to a tree. Nothing happened. He dashed thirty feet farther to a slab of rock, and waited an instant. Any time now, she was only over there a little way.

He Indianed it around the rock, and caught a glimpse of white at the edge of a rock. If she was there, he had her. He stepped out quickly, watching that edge of cloth, and just as he stepped into the open a rifle blasted.

He felt the hot burn of the bullet and sprang back, to see the girl standing there, fifty feet off in another direction.

Why, the dirty little——! Fooled him, fooled him like he was a youngster with an edge torn from her skirt.

And then he lowered his rifle.

She'd fooled him, all right, but she had missed, missed a clean shot. Sure, he'd burned his neck with the bullet and it would be raw and sore, but he'd have a woman to. . . .

"Bitner!"

It was a man's voice, conversational in tone, and it was behind him. He sprang like a cat, turning as he leaped, and when he hit the ground, his rifle——hers actually——was hosing flame. He staggered and something hit his wind a wicked blow, and he settled on his feet, flat on the rocks, and saw Radigan standing there, standing straight, his right side toward him like a blasted soldier at attention on the parade ground; like a man in a duel.

Bitner got his Winchester up and squeezed shut on the trigger and felt the rifle jump in his hand, but the recoil or something staggered him and, puzzled, he saw his bullet kick dust from the rocks between them. Well, by God, he'd . . . he was lying on his face on the cold rock, and the snow was blowing away from his face because he was breathing hard. He heard the dying echo of his shot. It sounded like two shots, and he got his knees under him and started to get up.

It was the blood on the mesa top that bothered him. Somebody was shot almighty bad, somebody was really bleeding like a stuck hog, somebody——the blood was there, around his knees and on the rock where he had been lying. His eyes had refused to focus but now they did and he saw it was his blood and he had been gutshot.

He had gutshot a man once and it had taken the fellow a long time to die.

Bitner used the rifle for a crutch and got to his feet. He could see the girl, looking like an angel in her white gown, walking from behind the rocks toward Radigan. It was that dress that had thrown him, right there at the beginning; in a place like that he had not expected to see anybody in a white dress, and before he got himself adjusted to it she had taken a cut at him and gotten away.

It was a hell of a way to die, over a woman he had only seen a time or two and who didn't want any part of him, anyway.

He was swaying on his feet, and wanting a shot at Radigan, but more than anything he wanted a bullet through the skull. He had always had guts enough, but did he have guts enough to die from a belly shot without crying like a baby? That man he had shot, he'd cried and screamed.

Something raw and horrible tore from his own throat, and he lifted the rifle and felt the slam of the bullet and knew he had won. He had won because he was dying, going, dead.

The last thing he remembered was lying with his cheek against the rock and remembering how he had helped his ma shave his pa after he had been killed. "A man shouldn't be buried like that," his ma had said. "He should face up to the Gates like a man, with his beard trimmed."

He had no son, so who was going to shave him? Who would fix his body for burial?

A man should have a son.

He saw his bloody hand lying inches before his eyes, the cold wind drying the blood on it, and he tried to open his mouth to tell Radigan that a man should have a son, and beyond that there was nothing further.

Gretchen had come to Radigan quickly. "You all right?" he asked. He asked it without looking at her, for he was watching Bitner. She knew the man was dying and Radigan knew it but he did not move his eyes from Bitner for even an instant.

"I'm all right," she said, "I was hoping you'd come."

"Sorry I was late."

"You weren't late. You were right on time."

Ross Wall came up to the house from the barn in the first bleak morning light. He stamped the snow from his boots and came in at Angelina's call. He held his hat in his hand, his blocky head looking like the head of a big grizzly in the shadow cast by the lamp.

"Ma'am, I want we should saddle up and ride out of here, right away this morning."

Angelina Foley felt something seem to turn over inside her. "What's happened?"

"Nothing yet. Nothing I know of, only Bitner didn't come back, and if Bitner doesn't come back, he's dead. It's another man gone, and one of the best."

"Is that all?"

"No," he said bluntly, "it ain't all. Not by a damn' sight."

If his other words had not impressed her, these did. It was the first time Ross Wall had ever sworn in her presence.

"It ain't all. There's strangers around, three or four of them. Mighty salty looking men, Gorman says. He came on three of them up in the trees last night; they just sat their saddles with Winchesters in their hands and looked at him. They didn't say I, yes or no, they just looked, and he looked back. Then Gorman rode back here and asked for his time."

"Is there more?"

"Yes. I never did cotton to what Harvey wanted to do I never liked him nor trusted him, nor saw what you and your Pa saw in him. He's brought you to trouble, and I'd like to see you out of it.

"Those men out there," he pointed. "I think they're waiting for him. I think he'll come back through the snow and he'll ride right up to here and they'll shoot him right out of his saddle.

"And that isn't all. The sheriff is down at San Ysidro. I don't mean Flynn, but Flynn's boss. Name is Enright, or something. He rode in yesterday with three deputies and he has been asking questions around, and one of those deputies has a horse with a Texas brand."

Angelina Foley walked to the fire and picked up the coffeepot. It was always a woman's way to turn to food in an emergency. Fix a hot meal, make coffee; it was a sensible way. And that was what she should be doing, making a hot meal for some man rather than trying to prove how smart she was and how she could run a cow outfit as well as any man. She had not even managed to run a home, not anywhere.

So all their fancy dreams of wealth were empty. All Harvey's confident talk, his striding up and down, his gestures—they were as empty as he was—all those big ideas from men who would rather steal than do an honest day's work with their fine contempt for men who did work. Fools, Harvey called them, hayshakers, so now where was he?

"Can we get out of here?"

For the first time she saw hope in Wall's eyes. "I think so. I think they'd be glad to be shut of us. We couldn't take anything, of course. Just personal stuff. But we could ride out, ma'am. . . ."

"Don't call me ma'am," she said irritably. "My name is Gelina."

They were coming down Vache Creek now, six of them, one with his skull tied in a bloody bandage, one with a broken arm, now in a sling. Their horses' hoofs dragged and the men slumped wearily in the saddle.

Harvey Thorpe was numb as well as exhausted. They were all numb.

The ride had been cold and they had been anxious to get on with the holdup. The stage showed up on time and they had ridden out and stopped it, confident of their numbers, confident of their guns.

Only the man on the box had a shotgun and he didn't drop it, he didn't hold up his hands. His first charge of buckshot had torn a man's face off and the second dropped a man, screaming. Amid plunging horses and wild shots he had coolly picked up a Winchester and opened fire. Other men were shooting from the stage itself and horses were down, men screaming, and Harvey Thorpe had been among the first to break into flight. A few miles away they had come together, and they had kept on going. And nobody had anything at all to say.

The thing none of them wanted to say was that the men they had called hayshakers, the men who worked for their money, had been ready for them.

What happened to the others Harvey never was to know. All he did know was that one man sitting up on the box of that stage had not thrown up his hands: he had simply opened fire. From then on it had been nightmare, pure nightmare.

It was not supposed to happen. Their guns were supposed to frighten the stage driver and express messenger into immobility while they were robbed. That was the way it was supposed to happen.

Harvey knew but one thing, and he knew deep within himself that when he heard that shotgun blast and saw that man's face vanish in a mask of blood, his own guts had turned to water.

They rode into the ranch yard and somebody said, "Harvey!" And it wasn't one of his own men.

The exclamation made him look up and he saw Radigan standing there in the middle of the ranch yard.

He was standing there with his hands empty, just waiting. And then Harvey saw Loren Pike in the barn door, and Charlie Cade at the corner of the corral, and lean, round-shouldered Adam Stark leaning against the doorpost of the house. And beside the corral and still farther away was John Child. And even a less wary man than himself would have read the story in their presence here, in their manner.

A man behind him said, "Count me out, Harvey," and Harvey Thorpe heard a gun drop into the dust. And behind him other guns dropped.

Harvey looked at Radigan and felt the hatred inside

himself like something raw and sore. Radigan had been nowhere near that stage, but suddenly it seemed as if Radigan had been the man on the box who lifted that shotgun. Without him everything would have been all right.

Out of the welter of thoughts left in his brain came a slow, cool knowledge that he could not win but he could still defeat Radigan. Alive, Radigan was the victor, but dead he was nothing at all, simply nothing.

"Gelina let you come here?"

"She's gone," Radigan said. "She rode out with Wall and a pack horse. Heading for California, I think."

So that was over, too.

Behind him he heard horses walking away, getting clear of him, and Radigan stood there, waiting. Nobody had asked him to drop his gun, nobody suggested he surrender.

Of course, within a few days they would know all about what happened in Colorado, and he would be a wanted man. It was strange he had not considered that, but all his plans had been predicated on success.

Why, they could hang him! And they might.

And Radigan, standing there with his feet apart, just waiting for him to draw and die.

"I'll be damned if I will!" Harvey said angrily. "You're all just waiting for me to make a move so you can kill me! I'll surrender! You think I'll hang, but I won't! I'll beat it! I can still win! I tell you—!"

He meant every word of it, believed it all. Why, so many things could happen in a trial, and he still had friends, he could still dig up some money, he'd show them, he'd . . .

Harvey Thorpe had no intention of drawing, but he did. He felt his hand dropping for the gun and something in his brain screamed that it was madness, he could not win, but he could kill Radigan, he could. . . .

"I didn't think he was going to, there at the end," Pike said. "I thought he was throwing in his hand."

"Even a coyote in a trap," somebody else said, "he'll snap at anything, just to hurt, to kill."

"How'd you guess, Tom?" Cade said. "Because you had to guess, it was that fast."

"Can we do anything for him?" That was John Child. "I mean, is it too late?"

"Sure," Pike replied, "the man's dead."

And he was.